A Rock and a Hard Place

Wes Markin

For Audrey and Douglas

Contents

About the Author   vii
By Wes Markin   ix
Praise for Wes Markin   xi

AND THEN THERE WERE NONE   1
IN THE COMPANY OF WOLVES   11
I LOVE NEW YORK   14
MOTHER'S RUIN   18
Chapter 1   25
Chapter 2   33
Chapter 3   44
Chapter 4   50
Chapter 5   61
Chapter 6   67
Chapter 7   76
Chapter 8   84
Chapter 9   95
Chapter 10   106
Chapter 11   114
Chapter 12   123
Chapter 13   131
Chapter 14   140
Chapter 15   152
Chapter 16   159
Chapter 17   165
Chapter 18   174
Chapter 19   182
Chapter 20   201
GONE BUT NOT FORGOTTEN   214
BETTER THE DEVIL   217

YOUR FREE DCI YORKE
QUICK READ   221
Also by Wes Markin   223
JOIN DCI EMMA GARDNER AS SHE
RELOCATES TO KNARESBOROUGH,
HARROGATE IN THE NORTH
YORKSHIRE MURDERS ...   225
Acknowledgments   227
Stay in touch   229
Review   230

About the Author

Wes Markin is the bestselling author of the DCI Yorke crime novels set in Salisbury. His latest series, The Yorkshire Murders, stars the compassionate and relentless DCI Emma Gardner. He is also the author of the Jake Pettman thrillers set in New England. Wes lives in Harrogate with his wife and two children, close to the crime scenes in The Yorkshire Murders.

You can find out more at:

www.wesmarkinauthor.com

facebook.com/wesmarkinauthor

By Wes Markin

DCI Yorke Thrillers

One Last Prayer

The Repenting Serpent

The Silence of Severance

Rise of the Rays

Dance with the Reaper

Christmas with the Conduit

Better the Devil

A Lesson in Crime

Jake Pettman Thrillers

The Killing Pit

Fire in Bone

Blue Falls

The Rotten Core

Rock and a Hard Place

The Yorkshire Murders

The Viaduct Killings

The Lonely Lake Killings

The Crying Cave Killings

* * *

Details of how to claim your **FREE** DCI Michael Yorke quick read, **A lesson in Crime**, can be found at the end of this book.

Praise for Wes Markin

"An explosive and visceral debut with the most terrifying of killers. Wes Markin is a new name to watch out for in crime fiction, and I can't wait to see more of DCI Yorke." – **Stephen Booth, Bestselling Crime Author**

"A pool of blood, an abduction, swirling blizzards, a haunting mystery, yes, Wes Markin's One Last Prayer has all the makings of an absorbing thriller. I recommend that you give it a go." – **Alan Gibbons, Bestselling Author**

"Cracking start to an exciting new series. Twist and turns, thrills and kills. I loved it." – **Ross Greenwood, Bestselling Author**

"Markin stuns with his latest offering... Mind-bendingly dark and deep, you know it's not for the faint hearted from page one. Intricate plotting, devious twists and excellent characterisation take this tale to a whole new level. Any *serious crime fan will love it!"* – **Owen Mullen, Best-selling Author**

Text copyright © 2022 Wes Markin

First published 2022

ISBN: 9798440388062

Imprint: Dark Heart Publishing

Edited by Brian Paone

Cover design by Cherie Foxley

AND THEN THERE WERE NONE

A s she took a mouthful of fruit tea, Lynna tried to keep her hand steady. A couple of drops splashed onto the oak table. She swallowed the blueberry-flavored liquid and sighed. The tremble wasn't from fear. It was from old age. In her formative years, she'd been able to spear a deer from a greater distance than any of her peers and had earned the nickname Longshot Lynna. Now she'd struggle to even lift that spear.

She stared at the plant pot in the center of the oak table —a gift from their new leader, Celestia. The previous week, it had been merely green shoots. This week, it had started to flower—flower how the Nucleus had once flowered. This was before, of course. Before Celestia's father, the late leader of the Nucleus, had sown his cancerous seeds.

Lynna looked between the two withered faces at the oak table: Jerusha and Pamelia. There were only three of them now. Before the Great Day of Burning, there had been five, but the eldest, Gillie, had perished in the flaming church, and Emmer had succumbed from a heart attack only days later.

1

Three remained.

Only three.

Such a small, small number.

"But enough," Lynna said, "to do what we must do."

Lynna waited. A response didn't come. She waited some more. It still didn't come.

Pamelia scarped at something on the oak table with a long nail.

Jerusha stared into his cup as he swirled his fruit tea round and round.

Lynna considered slamming her fist on the table to startle them all into agreement. But that was behavior from a time long ago. She was older and frailer now. So, instead, she weakly coughed, and said, "So we vote, and we vote now."

Scraping ...

"In the same way we voted for Merithew's fate."

Swirling ...

"Simply raise your hand if—"

"Last time we voted, there were five of us." Pamelia drew her fingernail back from the oak.

"And all five of us voted the same way," Lynna said. "It can still be like this. We can all vote the same way."

"But still," Jerusha said, pushing away his cup while regarding Lynna from the corner of his eye. "Five hands last time gave us that strong assurance that our decision was right."

"Some would still argue that it was the wrong decision." Pamelia looked up from the mark that had been bothering her on the table.

"It was the *right* decision." Lynna again resisted the urge to bang the table. "Merithew was a bad leader. His treatment of women was abhorrent. Althea, herself, would have sanctioned his execution, *even though* he was her direct descendent. Griffin, for all his failings, would have been a good transitional leader in terms of resurrecting the old ways. If it wasn't for that vile outsider, Frank Yorke, our call would have been a good one." She narrowed her eyes. "The vile outsider, I might add, that Celestia still keeps on our lands as some kind of bodyguard—"

Jerusha coughed, not deliberately. It was merely one of the signs of his ninety-year-old body deteriorating. After the coughing fit subsided, he apologized and said, "We do not need to have this discussion again." He paused to catch his breath. "I think we can all agree that if not for the crooked hand of fate and the malicious interferences of that outsider, Frank Yorke, Griffin would have justified *that* vote."

"And we all agree," Lynna continued, "that despite Celestia bringing back the equality between the sexes that Althea demanded, she is not fit to lead. She is too corrupted by outside influences. Their heinous media and rotten movies have influenced her, as has that vile outsider, Yorke! That education program brought in from Mossbark! I mean, really? We may as well collapse our borders and become part of their town! Anyway, like Jerusha said, we're repeating ourselves. We know what's coming to the Nucleus. Mossbark knows we're small now, that we are easy pickings. An altruistic leader such as Celestia will simply not do. We will fall so quickly. By delaying this vote, even for a minute, we are losing valuable time. So shall we do this?"

Pamelia sighed. "But we are so few, in this room. Althea always demanded we vote with five. I am stuck on this—"

"But you make no sense. Three hands here would give you the same assurances?" Lynna raised an eyebrow. "After all, three hands would have been enough to win a five-person vote, would it not?"

Pamelia and Jerusha nodded. The logic was reasonable. They would move only on a completely unanimous decision. Three votes.

"Ready?" Lynna asked.

"Yes," they both replied.

"Raise your hand if you agree Celestia should be removed as leader. And, just to be clear, removal of leader does require execution." She raised her hand. As enthusiastic as she was, she would have liked to straighten her arm completely, like a keen child in a classroom, but her arthritic elbow kept her zeal low key.

Pamelia and Jerusha stared at one another. Neither made a move.

Feeling her chest tighten, Lynna flitted her eyes between the two elders. She hadn't expected this delay. In all the discussions, they had been as convinced as her. Yet, here they were, like two gunslingers, teasing each other with their eyes, not revealing who would go for the draw first.

"I can only table the motion one more time—"

A heavy knock sounded at the cabin door.

Lynna turned her furious eyes to the door. "There is a council meeting in progress!" She was surprised by how loud she was. If the stakes of what was currently happening hadn't been so high, she may have cracked a smile over the strength that remained in her vocal cords. What was more, it had worked! There wasn't a second knock. She refocused on her indecisive gunslingers. "Raise your hand if you agree that Celestia should be removed as leader."

The knocking at the door had clearly jarred Jerusha into action. He raised a hand. She noted, with some jealousy, the flexibility he still possessed in his elbow.

4

All eyes were now on Pamelia. She'd resumed her scraping of God knows what on the table.

Come on, come on ...

It was three or nothing—

A second, *louder*, knock rapped at the door.

Lynna couldn't hold back any longer. She struck the table with her fist, hard enough for the plant pot in the center to do a little hop. Remarkably, she didn't feel any pain but knew she would probably pay for it later. She considered getting to her feet and admonishing the impatient person at the door but knew that by the time she hobbled over there, the pressure on Pamelia to cast the deciding vote would have subsided. "Ignore it." Lynna stared at Pamelia, who still scraped the table. "Pamelia, it is now or—"

Another knock. The most insistent of the three.

Lynna kept her eyes on Pamelia, willing her to stop scraping with that fingernail and take that hand into the air ...

And then it happened. The scraping stopped, and Pamelia's arm began a slow ascent.

Lynna wanted to whoop with delight; however, she refrained. It would be undignified behavior. "I count three votes—"

The door opened.

Lynna felt enough frustration in her old bones to get to her feet. She stared at the front door, ready to roll back the years and unleash fury onto the intruder.

No one entered.

Lynna eyed the two other elders who were both staring at the empty doorway, Pamelia having to turn around in her chair to do so.

"Who's there?" Lynna said. "Why do you disturb us?"

"The topic of your conversation." Celestia strode into the cabin.

Lynna and Jerusha shared an astonished look.

Celestia closed the door behind her and approached the end of the oak table. "Continue. Please. Don't let me interrupt these deliberations."

"Celestia," Lynna said, "your presence here is inappropriate. The council deliberates and reports to you, their leader, outside the chamber—"

"My presence here is inappropriate, then?" Celestia asked.

"Yes, with all due respect, Celestia, it is," Lynna said. "I thought you would know the ways from Merithew."

"My father, Merithew?" She touched the long oak table. "The man who built this oak table himself so you could deliberate around it for the good of the Nucleus?"

Lynna nodded. "Yes, Celestia. We always have the interests of the Nucleus at heart—"

"I'm guessing this is the table where you deliberated his death?"

Lynna had been standing for a minute now, so her back was aching, and her posture was deteriorating. She put a hand on the table to steady herself. "I don't know what you think you know, Celestia, but the discussions in this cabin are confidential until we report to—"

"Confidential?"

"Yes. That is our way."

"You have always been so protective of your ways, haven't you?"

"Our ways," Jerusha said, looking at his cup.

"Your ways," Celestia said.

"Your ways won't work here," Lynna said. "Look at you. All done up like one of the clowns from the outside world."

"I have yet to see a clown with black eyeliner and lipstick. A witch, maybe, but not a clown."

"A witch, a clown—it matters not," Lynna said. "These aren't our ways. Think of Althea."

"Althea was a long, long time ago."

"The length of time is insignificant in the great picture," Jerusha said, finally looking up at her.

"True. Time is certainly insignificant if we fail to learn from it," Celestia said.

"And now you sound just like your father." Lynna winced over the pain in her back, and so she eased herself into the chair.

"Actually," Celestia said, "I'm nothing like Merithew. You see, Merithew looked outside for the solution to the problems here. I, on the other hand, have looked inside."

"Oh really?" Lynna said. "Do enlighten us to where this problem is!"

"Here." She paused. "In this room."

Lynna smiled. "You've no idea."

Celestia nodded down at the plant pot. "Did you like your gift? It goes well with the table my betrayed father built for you."

"We expressed our appreciation already for that."

Celestia tucked her hair behind her ear and pointed to her black earpiece.

"What is that?" Lynna asked.

"It allowed me to sit in on the meeting with you. I know you wouldn't approve of using such modern technology, but we don't want to be left behind."

"I don't understand," Lynna said. And she still didn't, not really.

Jerusha sighed. "She bugged the plant pot."

"Maybe if you weren't still living in the eighteenth

century, you might have considered such possibilities, been a little more cautious, perhaps?"

"What do you want, Celestia?" Lynna asked.

"To lead. Without your interference if I so choose. It's my birth right."

"Your father relinquished your birth right when he betrayed our values."

"And I'm here to reclaim it from you."

"I thought you heard the conversation?" Jerusha curled his top lip. "You won't be reclaiming anything."

"Really?" Celestia reached into her leather jacket. "I wasn't aware that the deciding vote had been cast." She pulled out a gun. "I know you voted for my execution, Lynna, and you too, Jerusha. But I wasn't aware that Pamelia had cast her vote yet. Maybe she would see sense. Maybe she would convince you of the errors of your ways. Maybe"—she held up the gun—"I won't need this after all."

Lynna opened her mouth to speak, but nothing came out. A stunned silence surrounded the room, and Lynna realized she was central to that. She spied Jerusha's pale face and realized he would be of little help. She turned her twitching eyes onto Pamelia, who was looking rather unfazed, considering they would already be dead if Celestia had seen her hand in the air.

"So, let's recreate the scene." Celestia pointed the gun at Jerusha. "Hand in the air."

Jerusha obliged.

"And you, Lynna."

Lynna rose her bent arm.

"Higher."

"This is as high as it goes, you brat. Respect your elders."

"Like you respect your leaders, eh?"

Celestia turned the gun onto Pamelia. "So, Pamelia, what's it to be?"

Pamelia didn't look fazed by the threat. She kept her gaze on the mark that had kept her fingernail preoccupied. "Gillie died on the Great Day of Burning."

"I know," Celestia said. "And it hurts me. I loved her—"

"No, child. You didn't love her. Not like I loved her, at any rate. We were lovers nearly our entire lives."

Lynna heard Jerusha sit upright in his chair. He would be surprised by this revelation. She, herself, had suspected but had never sought out any confirmation. No one in the Nucleus would have frowned upon same-sex relationships, but having two elders from the council involved in an affair may have raised eyebrows. "This is all getting rather uncomfortable. Celestia, I suggest we all take time to cool our heads—"

"No," Pamelia said. "Celestia has come here for the truth, and she'll get it."

Lynna shook her head. *Don't be doing anything foolish now, Pamelia. Celestia is a cornered animal ...*

"The truth is, Celestia, I hesitated in casting my vote, because Gillie believed in you. She loved you. But I wavered, and before you entered this room, I started to raise my hand."

No, no, what are you doing, Pamelia?

"Why?" Celestia pointed the gun first at Lynna, then at Jerusha, "Did these two monsters pressure you?"

Pamelia shook her head and panned her gaze from the mark on the table to Celestia. "No, they didn't. I couldn't get over the fact that you brought an outsider into our world. That is what your father did and look what happened. And even then, I was still filled with doubt. But none remains now, Celestia. You bugged us and brought a gun into the council room! You are as poisonous as your father." She rose her hand. "So, I cast my vote."

Lynna dropped her hand. "No—"

Jerusha's head snapped to one side. The bullet's exit wound filled Lynna's eyes with blood.

Unable to see, she heard a second shot as she rubbed at her eyes. Then came the thumping of someone hitting the ground. *Pamelia.*

Tears forming in Lynna's eyes helped clear her vision. Celestia, currently a blurred silhouette, remained in the same position at the head of the table. "Everything we ever did, we did for the Nucleus."

"That's what my father said too," Celestia said. "And in a way, I understand him now, and I understand you too."

Lynna's eyes cleared, and the image of Celestia quickly became sharper, as did the gun in her hand, pointing directly at her. She gulped. "My advice to you is to never make it personal."

"I'm not."

Lynna heard the shot, then felt nothing else.

IN THE COMPANY OF WOLVES

Celestia placed the gun on the table in front of Jake.

Jake brushed aside his porridge and placed his large hand over the weapon. "I heard. I thought, *I hoped*, it was hunters."

"*The Godfather Part Two*."

"Not now, Celestia—"

"Michael's brother betrayed him, remember? He did what he had to do."

"It's *just* a film. What have you done, Celestia?"

She told him.

"Fuck," he said, taking his hand off the gun. He closed his eyes and felt his world spinning. Celestia, innocent and good, one of the only shining lights in the dark world he wandered.

A killer now.

Like him.

He opened his eyes. "This is my fault."

She threw the earpiece into his porridge.

"I was eating that."

"They were going to kill me. What was the alternative?"

"Come and tell me?"

"So you could take care of the little girl?"

Jake shook his head. "Isn't that the reason I'm still here? To take care of you?"

"No. You stayed here to heal."

He pointed to where his earlobe used to hang. "I'm healed. This isn't growing back."

"A shame," she sneered. "You looked better with it."

"And you looked better when you weren't psychopathic." He rolled his eyes and sighed. He looked down at the gun. She was starting to assert her independence in ways that didn't horrify him—he'd seen too much for that—but rather in ways that disappointed him. He wanted her to grow up to be everything he wasn't, and now she was behaving just like he'd done for so many years.

"What's done is done," she said.

"Yes. Do you need me to clean up the mess? Be your Winston Wolf?"

"No. *Pulp Fiction* is *just* a film," she sneered. "I want everyone to see what I've done. I've called my people to the square."

Jake stood. "And how do you think they'll respond? You were supposed to be bringing the good times back to the Nucleus, not more violence and death."

"I had to hit the reset button."

"You put bullets in it! And that rarely resets anything!"

"It was them or me, you know that. When you calm down, you'll realize—"

"I'd have found a way."

"It would have been exactly the same way."

He flinched. No point in arguing. She was probably right. "So, why am I still here? If not to be of use or to heal?"

Celestia looked away. "I like you."

Jake nodded. "Admittedly, I'm glad someone likes me. I've always been rather deprived in that department, but still not a reason for staying in a place I detest."

"You detest what the Nucleus was, not what it can be."

"Not true. A cult is a cult."

She scrunched her face.

"If you're staying, then it's your funeral." Jake stood. "I'm going to be moving on shortly."

Celestia shrugged and turned her back to him.

"After I ensure everything is okay here," he said. "Because, for my sins, I like you too."

I LOVE NEW YORK

Sheriff Gordon Kane's life was just like the
superglued 'I love New York' cup in his hand—
scarred with deep black lines but holding together.
Just. He raised the cup and looked at the underside. Not a
drop of liquid worked its way through the fault lines. He
added a hefty helping of whiskey to the coffee.

He looked between piles of dirty dishes and trash over-
flowing from the can. He felt the urge to clean, but two
burning mouthfuls of alcoholic coffee had wiped that out.
He filled his cup with neat whiskey this time and left the
kitchen.

A surge of irritation threatened his fuzzy feeling when
he bypassed the bedroom and saw Susan still at rest. Then
he headed into his study and approached the wall,
beholding the Nucleus in all its glory. Using drones, he'd
snapped every significant part of that insidious realm and
enlarged the images, assembling them in the correct position. He'd spent countless hours these last weeks, learning
the ins and outs of this small pocket of inhumanity, and if he
finally gained access, sorry, *when* he finally gained access,

he would be sure footed as he cleaned that place from top to bottom.

The Nucleus covered the entire back wall. He traced the Southernmost Forest with his finger, before standing on a stool and tracing the Northernmost Forest.

Gordon climbed down from the stool and headed to the Westside, where he'd circled in red marker the sentry box at the top of the hill that led up from Brady Crossing. Partway down the hill, his drone had snapped a burned-out vehicle at Netow bend. Pausing for some whiskey, Gordon worked across his map, taking his finger to a large cluster of wooden cabins he assumed to be a residential area. He bounced his fingertip off many of the cabins, making the sound of an explosion with each touch.

He smiled at the blackened skeleton of an old barn, which had been used, unsuccessfully, by Pastor Frederick Deering to try to bring religion to a devilish land.

With another mouthful of whiskey, he turned to another wall, in which he'd installed key players in this whole sorry affair. Many of them had *Deceased* scribbled beneath them, prompting another smile from him. He read the names of the dead: Merithew, Lemuel, Griffin, Frederick, Alton, Norman. He touched the remains of the face of the broad, shaven-headed woman he'd killed on the steps of his station. *Angelita.* Having no picture of her in life, he'd had to opt for a photograph of her corpse. Walker, the wolfish, white-haired man who'd marched alongside her to his station that night, was still alive and in Gordon's possession in a jailcell.

Gordon clapped his hands.

He'd turned the head of all those who berated him!

Pulling the trigger on that hillbilly, Angelita, had been the most significant moment of his existence, and now those who'd considered him insignificant, weak, cowardly even were forced to eat their words as he plotted a cleansing inferno that would sweep his world clean.

He drained the last of his whiskey and touched the faces of those still living.

Frank Yorke. An out-of-towner living among them and supporting them. Albert Hardy and Logan Reed, two men who had offered support to Yorke and were, therefore, of interest. And finally, Celestia. Merithew's daughter. The drones had shown her leading meetings in the town square. It made sense that she was their new leader.

He headed out of the study and into the bedroom. He scowled at Susan lying there, then turned to the full-length mirror in the corner of the room.

He observed her in the reflection. "You continually cheated on a man, who became a soldier, who will soon be a hero."

He refocused on his own self and peeled off his T-shirt. He prodded his large gut, which rippled.

"Hardly the Hollywood superstar," Susan said.

Gordon turned. "For a man in his late fifties, it could be worse."

"Better ... worse ... it doesn't matter. You're a fat fuck, Gordon. And I'll always know who you are, no matter what you do."

Alcohol often made people angrier. In his job in law enforcement, Gordon had a fair amount of experience of this. But alcohol had never really brought out the demons in him.

"Why did you come back, Susan?"

"Because you made me!"

"No ... I don't believe that. You came back because of what I did to that woman from the Nucleus. You saw what I

16

was capable of." He stepped toward the bed, undoing his belt. "And I know you, Susan. I know what you crave. That limelight, that sparkle. After tolerating a sap for so long, you weren't about to miss out on what was due to you."

"You talk as if you are about to go onto the walk of fame, you fat fuck!"

He peeled off his trousers and underwear, lifted the bedsheet, and slipped in behind her. "Who knows? One day I might be," Gordon said with a smile. "There's film potential here, surely. I'll take down that rotten cult, and the whole world will know who did it." He nestled in behind her. She was cold to the touch. *Nothing new there, then.* "Turn and face me."

"No. You sicken me."

"Suit yourself." He ran his hand down the front of her body, between her ample breasts, over her rounded stomach, before stroking the mound of hair between her legs. He worked his fingers, even though she offered him no response. His own desire grew though, and his erection pressed against her back. "Not even a sound? You used to enjoy this, enjoy being with me. So much. What happened, Susan?"

"You happened."

He worked harder. "Not even a quiver. A single gasp. Do you hate the man you left so much?"

"I do."

He rolled her onto her back and looked into her wide eyes. He stroked her grey face, rubbing his fingertips over the dried bullet hole in the center of her head.

"One day you will be proud of me, Susan, and one day you will love me again."

He leaned in and kissed her.

MOTHER'S RUIN

Corrie looked between her two children.

Baby Inez was swaddled, so only her small, grey face was exposed. She lay, unmoving, in a hole in the earth beside a mound of dirt that was about to lock her away from the world of the living forever.

Marston, fourteen years old, and his sister's killer sat beside the grave, clutching his knees, rocking back and forth, muttering to himself. Vomit ran down his chin—the result of the poison he'd ingested.

"Keep drinking." Corrie nodded at the bottle of water that lay beside him.

He continued to rock, lost to whatever war was playing out deep in his own head. This wasn't pretence. In the past month, he'd been forced to impregnate a kidnapped outsider. He'd developed feelings for the victim, so when she'd been ruthlessly murdered, his control, his connection to reality had crumbled in on itself. Lost and desperate, he'd prepared a cocktail of deadly herbs this very morning and infected Corrie's and Inez's breakfast.

Stupid boy.

He hadn't used enough of the cocktail to kill Corrie and himself. She stared down at Inez's little white face.

Only this poor creature had paid the price of his foolishness.

"Drink, Marston."

But, of course, he didn't. And she acknowledged, with a sigh, she would have to force more down his throat after the burial.

As she used a spade to scoop the dirt up and over Inez, she forced back tears, believing that if she kept the anguish inside, it would fester. And festering despair would certainly provide the strength and resilience for revenge.

Merithew, deceased leader and descendent of the founder, Althea, had destroyed her entire world.

To begin with, Merithew had forced the child Inez, born to a kidnapped outsider onto Corrie, and she had done what was asked of her. She'd even come to love the child. And her reward? The use of her son's seed to the detriment of his mind—and the betrayal of her own husband, Sumner, when he'd tried to sacrifice their adopted child to the new leader, Griffin.

Corrie had ensured that Sumner had paid the ultimate price at her hands, but she wouldn't do the same with Marston. He was as much a victim of the old order of the Nucleus.

No, it was those who led the Nucleus who had to pay.

And there was only one place left to exact that cost.

The descendent Celestia.

* * *

After burying Inez and flushing out their stomachs some more, Corrie left Marston to his despondency and headed into the cabin. She cut her hair as short as she could and spent some time sharpening one of Sumner's old razors.

After shaving her head, she looked at herself in the mirror. Corrie was no more. Yes, she would allow everyone to use that name to make what was coming all the easier, but inside that identity was a sign of weakness. It represented a time when she had been accepting of rule. When she had wanted to be a good citizen and a good mother. The change of appearance would remind her that this was no more, while the name would continue to provide the ruse that she bled for the Nucleus, that she bled for Celestia.

She examined her face, pale and gaunt from the poison but still comprised of strong lines and creases. A drop of blood ran down her forehead and settled in her eyebrow. She checked the razor in her hand and saw the blood on the blade. She tilted her head and examined the bloody nicks on her baldness and grinned.

Outside, around the Focus, she heard the people leaving their cabins. Celestia had called a meeting at the square.

She stopped by her back garden to collect Marston, who still sat, muttering, by his baby sister's grave. "You'll be expected too."

Marston's battle with his demons continued.

She approached and knelt beside him, realizing only then that she was still holding the bloody razorblade. She looked between his trembling features and the stained steel. She leaned closer so she could pull his sweaty head to her shoulder. She ran her fingers through his damp hair. "My child, I'm so sorry for what has happened to you."

He continued to mutter.

"You do not deserve this torment." From the corner of her eye, she again saw the bloody razorblade in her hand. She tightened her grip on him, nuzzled her own face against his forehead, and kissed him. "You will heal, I promise you, Marston." She released him and stood. "We both will."

* * *

Corrie would be the first to admit that she was festering. *However, what did the outsiders call this place?* She scanned the small crowd. *The Rotten Core?* The festering here, in these old woods, far surpassed the festering in her own soul.

And here was evidence of that. Celestia, chosen one—or rather, spoiled brat—dripped with black makeup and a naivety that filled Corrie with more nausea than the poison her son had fed her this morning.

Celestia pranced before her dwindling people, justifying more bloodshed. The elders! The bitch had had the gumption to march into their meeting and execute all three of them.

She surveyed the pathetic crowd. Only thirty-seven residents remained in the Nucleus. Actually, make that thirty-four now that the elders were dead. Add to that, the fact that twelve residents were children, making this crowd of twenty-two very uninspiring.

Weakness.

That was what Corrie saw all around her.

A spineless, rotten core.

No one had spoken when Merithew brought organized religion and outsiders to their world. No one had breathed when his successor, Griffin, asked that their half-bred children be murdered. The only thing that wasn't weak around here, Corrie realized, was the large skulking stranger from another world—Frank Yorke.

Sensible move, Celestia, Corrie thought. *Making that killer your bodyguard.*

It was this bodyguard who had wired up a speaker and was now playing the highlights of the Elders' meeting.

Gasps and nervous chatter erupted from the gullible crowd. The betrayal had stunned them. It made them love and cherish their new queen even more.

Corrie rolled her eyes.

The stupidity of these people never ceased to amaze her.

She wanted to scream out, *"Do you not see what was happening there? The elders, for all their ridiculous past decisions, have your best interest at heart? Yes, Griffin was a mistake, but at least they knew Althea's line couldn't continue! Merithew destroyed the fabric of your world, and this is his daughter! His daughter! She will open your borders, and she will destroy you all!"* But she didn't scream anything.

She had to bide her time, because these people around her were desperate for salvation, and Celestia was making a good show of offering that.

This was a show. Nothing more.

She looked around the people again, all dressed in their cotton garments, large and well-fed from hunting, and the money that came from crime in other, faraway communities. She curled her top lip again.

It wasn't just Celestia who was spoiled; you all are! None of you know what it is like to struggle. Those generations have long passed. The whole sorry saga with Merithew and Griffin have given us an opportunity to change for the better, and you snub it! Snub it for this pretentious little bitch, who has just reduced your population to an even more manageable size for your enemies!

She paused to listen to Celestia.

"I know this is a shock. I cannot describe to you my feelings today after doing what was necessary, because I, too, feel the same confusion as you. These are different times, very different times to anything our kind has ever experienced before. But that doesn't mean we can turn and hide from it."

Everyone here is hiding. Everyone.

"By assassinating your rightful leader, not only would the elders have held us back from seizing opportunities for change, but they would have left you vulnerable to those changes. It is best we are strong when this change comes, to embrace *it* rather than let *it* embrace us."

Your father embraced change, remember? How did that end for him?

"But even in embracing these changes, we should not forget who and what we are, where we came from—our DNA."

Cute.

"So, that's why I'm going to ask you now for Hamlin Smith's minute, the child who tragically lost his life in the glade, so his mother, Emma Smith, could begin anew as Althea, our founder."

Tug on those heart strings, Celestia. And let me tell you now that I have begun anew. In fact, let it be a warning to you ...

Everyone lowered their heads to pay their respects.

At first, Corrie tilted her head. It was essential that she blend in, but the minute seemed to last a painful amount of time, so she submitted to irritation before the end and raised her head. Her eyes locked with Celestia's. *Why aren't you lowering your head, girl? Maybe I'm not the only one struggling with what we stand for?*

They held each other's gaze until Celestia ended the silence. "Thank you all for that single minute." Celestia took her eyes from Corrie and swept them over the crowd. "But the single minute has passed, and the single tear has been shed, so that is where we stop."

The words. Wow. I did underestimate you. Your arrogance is so extreme that you call on Althea's actual words!

"If we continue too far down the path of sentiment, then we are in danger of becoming like the dark and decrepit world we have left behind. One full of religion, control, and pain."

Look at you all, staring up at her in awe! You really are the crowd pleaser, Celestia.

"In our land, there is only one thing to believe in." Celestia pressed her fist to her heart, and the people did the same.

Together, they chanted, *"Us. The heart. The Nucleus."*

Still struggling from the effects of the poison and the nauseating performance, Corrie vomited down her front.

Fortunately, no one seemed to notice.

1

Jake and Logan embraced at the door of Celestia's cabin.

"A much more pleasant welcome than the last time I was here," Logan said, referring to being held at gunpoint at the sentry hut. He nodded at Celestia. "I appreciate the change in order."

Celestia's flinch was subtle, but Jake noticed it. The *change in order* had come about due to the death of the previous two leaders, one of whom was Celestia's father, so Logan's comment lacked tact.

Mind you, Logan was all about lacking tact, and Celestia knew that already, so she shook it off and said, "You're always welcome here, Logan, after how you saved Jake."

Jake patted the squat man on the shoulder. "Saved is a strong word. Preferred to go with lent a hand to, if that's alright."

"Well, I'm always glad to lend a hand when someone has a knife to their throat and looks rather helpless. Now, you going to leave me on the doorstep or offer me some of the local delicacies: plant tea, perhaps, and a leg of freshly speared roast pig?"

Jake stepped aside. "For a man who lives for stereotyping, offending, and general anti-social behavior, how can I refuse?"

As Logan passed, he pointed up at Jake's ear. "Just so we know, I wasn't around to save him when that happened. Which is good, because rats make me squeal like a little girl."

"As opposed to a little boy?" Jake said.

"Why does everything offend you, big man?"

"Because I wasn't born in Victorian England."

"I would have fit in well there."

"You don't fit in well anywhere, Logan."

"Fair point. Anyway, I think you wear the scar well. Never did picture you with an earring."

"I'm going to excuse myself from this banter between two insecure men, if that's okay?" Celestia said. "I've seen enough film noir to know who's really in charge here." She winked.

"Couldn't agree more. My wife was always in charge," Logan said.

"How did she control you?" Celestia asked.

"She kept me locked away."

Celestia exited the cabin, turned, and winked again through the open door. "Sounds like a good idea. It could be arranged ..."

"No thanks!" Jake said, waving her off. "A flying visit will do just fine."

Celestia turned and waved over her shoulder. "Jake, I'll see you later."

Jake flinched over the use of his real name and closed the door. He waited for Logan to question it, but he was too busy wandering around the cabin now and, fortunately, appeared to have missed it.

"Quite bare in here, Frank."

"One way of looking at it. Although people here would just say your home is cluttered."

"But no television? Clutter is one thing, but this is just deprivation!"

"Actually, she does have a TV. Logan, why the sudden visit anyway?"

"Food first. Serious discussion later."

Jake satisfied Logan's craving for meat with a venison sandwich. "It's not all about plant tea and roasted pig up here, you know," Jake said, sitting opposite him.

"Don't tell me you're starting to warm to the place."

"No," Jake said. "They're just not savages, is all I'm saying."

Logan raised an eyebrow. "You've forgotten what happened here?"

"They had their ways, yes, but all cultures have their ways."

"They fed people to rats."

"Admittedly, some ways are harder to stomach than others, but things are different now." He paused, recalling Celestia's assassination of three elders. "At least, will be, eventually, I think ... I *hope.*"

"I'm glad your favorite cult is starting to move in the right direction, Frank, but I'm here to say goodbye."

"You already did that. *Twice.*"

"No. This time is serious. I'm not coming back to Moss-bark again. It's not healthy."

"You and Cindy had another fight?"

"You could say that. She's gone back to her husband."

"I'm sorry to hear that."

"Don't be. It's for the best. She wasn't good for me. And a drifter like me certainly wasn't any good for her." He looked down at the table. "A man infatuated with his dead wife."

"Nothing wrong with that, Logan. I'm sure your wife appreciates the fact that you adore her, wherever she may be."

"In the ground, Frank. Let's not get sentimental."

Jake raised his eyebrows. "Okay ... I won't."

"Point is, this place is not healthy. Hell, my job as a rig driver is not healthy. I'm going home to work and mourn my wife properly, instead of trying to find happiness bedhopping around small towns in the middle of nowhere."

Jake held his hand up to silence him. "Wait ..." He cupped a hand to his ear. "I think I just heard all the womenfolk of New England simultaneously crying out in despair."

Logan laughed. "Nothing ever serious with you, is there? Unless someone is trying to kill you ..."

"Have you seen these wrinkles? I've had my fair share of serious!"

"I know, Frank ..." He paused. "Or is it Jake?"

Jake sighed. "Celestia slipped up there."

"At least give me some credit for spotting it, eh? You just see a fat, stupid truck driver!"

"Never gave much thought to the fat. Maybe to the stupid. But to be honest, I was too hung up on the misogynism and borderline racism."

Logan snorted. "I'm not surprised. A man from nowhere, hiding, will never give his real name, will he?"

"Well, I did before, and it backfired on me."

"What's your story, Jake? We've come far enough together now, surely? I'm rather offended that you never shared it with me."

"Don't be. It's not that I don't trust you, Logan. I know you've got my back. It's just that telling you won't achieve anything, apart from boring you, perhaps. I also don't want to put you in danger. Other people, who got to know me back in Blue Falls, paid for it with their lives."

"I'm not a man who scares easily."

"I know. I met Cindy."

Logan laughed. "So, tell me your story."

So, Jake told him.

* * *

Jake's story must have been interesting, because it kept Logan from his sandwich.

A few times during the tale, Jake paled, and at one point, he started to shake and had to excuse himself from the table to pace back and forth. When Jake reached his conclusion, he was moved to tears. "Article SE only wanted me. I was stupid to think I could ever hide from them. If I'd given myself to them, my friends would still be alive. And Piper? Shit. I'll never see her again."

"What about your family back home? Are they safe?"

Jake nodded. "I think so. I have a friend, the best there is, looking out for them. I don't think Article SE would be stupid enough to move on them; it would bring them too much attention."

"How often do you speak with your family?"

"Not often. And when I do, it's usually with my son, as my ex-wife wants nothing to do with me. It's been a while since I checked in. There's no cellphone reception in these woods, and I haven't dared to leave Celestia alone."

"Well, that was quite a story."

"And?"

Logan sighed and squeezed his best friend's shoulder. "And I think I'd be safer switching your name back to Frank."

Jake smiled. "Always thinking of number one!"

"If I was always thinking of number one, I wouldn't be sitting across from you with an offer on the table."

"What offer?"

"Did I not mention it?"

"No. You got stuck at the part where you vowed to stop populating the Northeastern states with illegitimate children."

Logan waved his hand. "Forget that. Been there. Done that. Bought the T-shirt. I've got some money. I've been saving for a while. It isn't much, but it will be enough to buy a small property. You see where I'm going with this?"

"Don't be offended if I say I've got no fucking idea!"

"A motorcycle repair shop!"

"Yes. That's quite an unpredictable leap."

"Do you want to open a motorcycle repair shop with me?"

Jake guffawed. He sat up straight in his chair. "Did you just listen to anything I just said?"

"Yes. Intently. Which is why I consider it best that you now look for a quiet life."

"That's what I've been trying to do."

"Badly, by the sounds of it. And it doesn't get much noisier than the Nucleus."

"Yes, but like I said, I'm worried about Celestia; she means a lot to me."

"This is the problem: your knack of discovering people who mean a lot to you. Maybe you need to start being less ... I don't know ... friendly?"

"What, like you? Offering me a home and a job despite barely knowing me?"

"Seems like your goodwill is infectious." Logan finally took a bite of his sandwich. "You're going to turn me down, aren't you?"

"Yes, but I appreciate the offer."

"You should do it. I just offered to save your life."

"I've made it this far."

"Every cat runs out of lives. But when the dust settles, would you reconsider?"

Jake shook his head.

Logan looked disappointed. "So, what will you do?"

"I don't know, Logan. Right now, I feel stuck between a rock and a hard place. If I leave Celestia, I risk leaving her in danger. Her people claim to adore her, but look at recent events, when things aren't to their liking, they quickly turn. Hopefully, if I stay, she'll eventually see sense, and I can get her away from here."

"So, that's the rock. What's the hard place?"

Jake sighed. "The hard place is home, Logan. My son. The real Frank. I need to see him. I need to be with him. But what happens if I go home?"

Logan shrugged.

"Precisely. And I can't risk that. I can't risk Frank."

"So, stuck between the Nucleus and a world you've fled from?"

Jake nodded.

Logan pointed up. "Then the only way is up, literally as well as figuratively. Let me carry you away from both worlds into the Yorke and Reed Motorcycle repair shop."

"I don't even know anything about motorcycles."

"Neither do I. That's what makes the project very exciting."

"Or foolish."

Logan finished his sandwich and pulled a hip flask from inside his leather jacket. "A farewell drink?"

Jake provided two mugs, and Logan poured them both a whiskey.

"Well, we may as enjoy our final chat," Logan said.

"There's a first time for everything."

"Park it. I'm going to miss you. Ever since you came into that diner and told me what a prick I was, things have improved."

Jake looked astounded.

"Well, maybe not regarding health and safety, but in terms of friendship. Been a long time since I had a friend."

"You've been a good friend, and I owe you my life, remember?"

"Hard to forget. I lied to you before. That's the first person I ever killed."

"I know."

"It changes you."

"I know that too."

"I won't be doing it again. It wasn't for me."

"It's a wise decision."

"How many people have you killed, Frank?"

Jake looked away. "Too many now."

"I guess it gets easier."

Jake sighed. "Unfortunately, yes. It does. But that's not a good thing, is it?"

2

Sheriff Gordon Kane stepped away from the man crumpled on the prison cell floor, shaking his bruised hand.

Deputy Scott Derby came up alongside him and put a hand on his boss's arm. "He's old, Sheriff."

"As am I, son." Gordon stepped forward and drove his boot into Walker's stomach.

The soldier from the Nucleus folded up on the floor, desperately sucking back air.

"So, an old man beating on an old man, kind of evens things out, don't you think?" Gordon asked.

Scott gripped his boss's arm this time. "I'm worried you're going to kill him, sir."

Gordon looked sideways and up into the face of his tall deputy. "Did you hear what he called me?"

Scott nodded.

The pummeled man on the floor laughed. "I called you a pussy." He snorted and spat blood on the floor. "A washed-up, lonely, *old* pussy."

Gordon sighed, looked at Scott again, and shrugged. "You see the situation?"

"I do, Sheriff. Please let me and Brad handle it. *Calmly.* We'll make sure he doesn't die."

"Calmly?" Gordon glanced at Scott's twin brother, who was fiddling with his ponytail—the only feature that distinguished him from his shaven-headed brother. "Brad?"

"Yes, Sheriff?"

"Do I look calm to you?"

Brad gulped. He fiddled harder with his ponytail.

"Brad?"

"Yes, Sheriff?"

"Calm?"

"Yes, Sheriff."

He turned back to Scott. "You see? Nothing to worry about. We're all on the same page."

"Sheriff—"

"And ..." Gordon plucked Scott's hand from his arm. "This man marched to my station, armed, and threatened my life, and all your lives too. So, do you think I give a rat's ass whether he lives or dies?"

"*Pussy!*"

"And there it is, the sound of us getting nowhere. Time to turn up the heat." Gordon approached Walker and knelt beside him.

Walker's left eye was swollen closed; his white facial hair was blood stained from his leaking nose.

"Not bad for a pussy, eh?" Gordon asked.

"There's three of you," Walker said, blood dribbling from the corner of his mouth. "And you haven't fed me well in days. Hardly a fair fight."

"But it began fairly enough though, didn't it, Mr. Walker? You and, what was she called again? Angelita, wasn't it? Strolling up to my station for a gunfight. Yet, you weren't quite ready for what was here, were you? What was it she asked me before I shot her? Have you ever killed anyone? She got her answer, didn't she? Didn't pay to underestimate me, did it? Maybe you should heed that as a warning."

Walker laughed. "You're a pussy. You shot Angelita because you had to. It was kill or be killed. You don't have the guts to kill an unarmed man. This is all for show ... So, pussy, the answer is no, once again. I'm not taking you home with me. You want to get into the Nucleus, you go yourself. Just keep an eye out for those bear traps. They're bad for your health."

Gordon eased himself into a sitting position beside Walker's head. "My offer still stands. You get us in, and you get to walk away and start afresh."

"I won't be walking anywhere but back here, Gordon, to scrape the flesh from your bones."

"Scrape? Nice image." Gordon smiled. "Is that how you savages operate up there in the woods?"

"Go up and take a look. Just watch where you step ..."

Gordon sighed and regarded the identical twins by the sliding cell door. "Don't worry, boys, I'm still calm. Patience of a saint. However"—he looked back down at Walker—"be warned. Every man has a limit."

Walker's long white hair, also blood stained, was glued to his sweat-stained cheeks. Gordon leaned forward and peeled it away.

"Get your hands off me," Walker said.

Gordon placed his hand tightly over the center of his prisoner's face, blocking off his nose. Walker reached up to push away the sheriff's hand, but he'd had the energy smacked out of him, and he struggled to move it.

"Relax ..." Gordon said. "You can still breathe through your mouth, can't you?"

"Get ... the ... *fuck—*"

Gordon rubbed the heel of his hand over his prisoner's entire face, smothering it with the blood from his nose. The sheriff worked his hand hard on his cheeks, before moving to his forehead, filling his wrinkled lines. Gordon withdrew his hand and eyed the blood-stained man.

"I thought you were a soldier, Walker." Gordon rose to his feet. "But I see a man wallowing in his own piss, shit, and blood."

"You'll find out, Gordon, what I am. One day, soon, you'll find out."

Gordon kicked Walker in the side of his face, snapping his head left.

Walker dragged his head straight again, panting and dribbling blood. "The flesh from your bones," he hissed.

"Can you all just shut the fuck up in there!" It was Leo Rayner, spending yet another day in the drunk tank next door to this cell.

Leo's contribution to Brady Crossing consisted mainly of fighting and drinking, but he was also known to try his hand at thievery. He didn't seem to mind spending most of his time in a cell, as the conditions were preferable to the stinking bedsit he festered in on the outskirts of town. "How is a man supposed to sleep in here?"

Gordon looked back at his deputies. "Shut him up."

Brad nodded and headed to the adjacent cell; Scott hung back.

"You keeping an eye on me, Scott?"

Scott shook his head.

Gordon refocused on the snivelling wreck on the cell floor. "You're a tough nut to crack, Walker, but every nut can be cracked. Just takes a little time. I'll be back tomorrow, to see if we can finally split your shell."

Walker laughed. "See you tomorrow, pussy."

As Gordon exited the cell, he glanced at Scott. "Feed him tonight. I don't want him dying when I take another run at him tomorrow."

* * *

"Is this trying to convince me to stay?" Jake asked.

"I don't know what you mean," Celestia said, looking through binoculars.

"You know exactly what I mean, Celestia." Jake put his hand on the binoculars and took them gently from her. He looked through them and sighted Thaxton, Everlyn, and several other soldiers of the Nucleus trudging toward the Southernmost Forest, armed with thick waste bags to dispose of the bear traps. He lowered the binoculars. "Disarming the Nucleus."

Celestia stared at him. "And how many fortified towns have you been in, Jake?"

"It's a ridiculous question. The Nucleus is not your run-of-the-mill town."

"No ... not yet."

Jake put his hands to his face, rubbed at it, and sighed.

"Why can't we be a normal town, Jake? We're human beings! The mistake of my ancestors was to separate us from the world. That's where the danger comes from. I aim to put that right."

Jake dropped his hands. "I understand your motivation. And, in a way, you're completely right. While the Nucleus cuts itself off from humanity, it will always be *the rotten core*. But please, listen to me. This is too fast! You have only just calmed the situation here. And by calming it, you had to execute three people! We've seen the drones overhead. Mossbark knows you're weak. Those bear traps, as much as they disgust me, were the last line of your defense. Why leave yourself completely vulnerable?"

"Look over there." Celestia pointed toward the skeleton of a new windmill that Thaxton was in the process of building and would eventually help power the Nucleus. "And over there." She pointed toward the beginnings of a new school building. "We are developing, expanding, our community is going forward not backward. The bear traps, the elders, the violence—that is not what we'll be about anymore. And my people support me. You see that. You have seen their faces as they listen to me."

"There's daggers in men's smiles."

"Sorry."

"It's a quotation I remember from school. William Shakespeare. You don't know if you can trust all your people."

"I know that. I will remain vigilant."

"So, remain vigilant with your defenses up! Settle the Nucleus before trusting those in your neighboring towns, because I'm warning you now, the world outside is full of people who can't be trusted."

"You think I don't know that?" Celestia turned from him.

"You are young and—"

She turned with her eyes wide. "Don't be condescending."

"I'm not. Your knowledge of the world comes from movies. I've lived in it. I'm telling you that if you lower your defenses, you will welcome in those who want to end you. And if they don't succeed, the people within your community will feel betrayed and turn on you anyway, just like they did with your father."

Celestia jabbed her finger at him. "My father was a monster. I am anything but."

"History is full of passionate monsters. It's hard to see clearly when completely driven, completely consumed."

"And what does that mean?" Her voice was rising in volume now.

"It means, be patient. I agree with your vision, but this is too fast, too emotional. Too impetuous. The community that you want can be built, but it must be measured, and the foundations must be strong."

"I am grateful to you, Jake, I really am. I wouldn't be here if it wasn't for you. But soon, I am going into Mossbark to ask that we become an official town in this county. I cannot do that with bear traps and guards. No, I'm sorry. My mind is made up."

Jake shook his head. "This is too dangerous."

"Then, leave. I love you. You know that. I want you to stay, but no longer can I look you in the eyes, *anyone in the eyes*, if we continue to be what we once were."

"Which is?"

"Evil, Jake. Evil, pure and simple."

* * *

HARDY'S CONVENIENCE STORE EST 1854.

Gordon looked up at the sign, then down the crumbling exterior which surely hadn't seen a lick of paint since the day it had been established. He grinned over some fond memories. As a child, Gordon's reward for being the best friend of Albert Hardy, the store owner's son, was a free soda every time he crossed this threshold. As an old man,

Gordon knew that no such reward awaited him, even though his once-upon-a-time best friend was now the store owner.

Sure enough, when he crossed the threshold, he was met with, "What do *you* want?" Albert was reading from a book on his counter.

"If that's how you greet your customers, you might need another trip to the library. I suspect you're going to get through a lot of books."

"Good. I like reading."

Gordon entered with his hands in the air. "Look, I come in peace."

"Don't worry, I'm not going to shoot you. I don't want to splatter the magazines. I wouldn't be able to sell them after."

Gordon laughed and lowered his hands. "At least you held onto that sense of humor in your grotty old age."

"You've known me for close to sixty years, Gordon. When did you ever know me to have a sense of humor?"

Gordon tutted and shrugged. "Come on, Alb. I thought we'd put the past behind us the other month, back at the station?"

Albert guffawed. "Did you?" He pulled off his reading glasses and dropped them on his book. "You shot someone from the Nucleus, and you're now supposed to be my biggest hero?"

"Well, you never liked them, did you?"

Albert narrowed his eyes. "An understatement. I've hated them for a long fucking time. While, all that time, you've been their biggest supporter."

"It wasn't like that, and you know it. My hands were tied."

Albert shook his head. "Oh, this is brilliant, Gordon! The sheriff's hands were tied against criminality!"

"In a way, yes."

"I'll ask one last time, before I return to my book; what do *you* want?"

"I want you to help me." Gordon approached the counter.

Albert raised an eyebrow and smirked. "What with? Some DIY equipment? Some stationery?"

"No, something that might get your old juices flowing."

"Your resignation and disappearance into obscurity?"

"How about helping me take down the Nucleus?"

Albert stood up straight. A smile crept across his face. "I'm aware that it can be quite common for people of a certain age, like us, to lose this." He put a finger to his head. "But I have to say I'm still surprised."

Gordon smiled back. "What do you say? Let's take down the rotten core together."

"You're serious, aren't you?"

"Deadly."

"Two old men taking down the Nucleus?"

"Absolutely."

"You looked in the mirror recently, Gordon? You're not Butch Cassidy, and I'm far from being the Sundance kid."

"They're not what you think they are."

"And what are they, then?"

"Weak. Weaker than they've ever been. They can't be more than three dozen, and a fair chunk of them are children."

Albert wagged a finger between them. "Still a lot more than two."

"They'll be more than two of us, Albert. Many more."

"Who?"

"Look around you. Your neighbors in their fancy shops.

The money has stopped. They're pissed. They're ready to remove the scourge on our land."

"Are they? Have you run it by them?"

"No, but I can feel it ... It's only a matter of time before their businesses collapse."

"And how'll decimating the Nucleus help with that?"

"Makes them feel better. It'll also make Mossbark attractive to outside investors without this malignant influence at its center."

"And attractive to drug dealers too?"

"There's a cost to any successful town."

"More crime that you'll turn a blind eye to?" Albert asked with a smirk.

"I'll cross that bridge when I come to it."

"Sounds like you don't need me. Just go and deputize the pissed business owners."

"No, I need you, Albert. You resisted their influence and refused their money. Everyone here has quiet respect for that."

"Everyone here got rich in that quiet respect."

"Yes. And now they realize the state of their foundations. They're ready to listen to you, and to me."

"It's an interesting proposal," Albert said, tapping his lip. "Very interesting indeed." He put on his reading glasses and picked up his book. "But no. I'm out."

"You hate them more than anyone—after what happened all that time ago, after what they took from you."

"Yes, it's true," Albert said, turning a page. "I have more reason than anyone to hate them, but the answer is still no."

"At least tell me why?"

"Because," Albert said, who still appeared to be reading, "that ship has long sailed. There was a time when I wanted you to step up to the plate, and I would have followed you into the fire, Gordon, but you opted for the status quo."

"I *protected* you. I let you continue even when I knew you were angering the Nucleus by refusing their money."

Albert smiled. "Look around. You want me to be grateful? Good day, Gordon."

"Is it because of that outsider, Frank Yorke? He lives there now. I've seen it on the images."

"I don't know what you're talking about, Gordon."

"You are making a mistake, Albert. This is what you've always wanted. One way or another, their time is coming to a close, but you, old man, you could make it so much smoother."

Albert looked up from his book. "Thanks for dropping by, Sheriff. Grab a soda on the way out for old times' sake."

3

While Gordon was out, Scott received a report of an abandoned vehicle on the outskirts of Mossbark. Scott asked his brother Brad to accompany him.

Brad, who was the better driver of the two, took the wheel and handled the bumpy road out of town with patience. En route, he touched on a taboo subject. "The sheriff is right, though. He does seem calm. Maybe we should trust him when he says he knows what he's doing?"

"I don't know ... That's just his way, always has been. I've known him for longer than you, little brother, and I tell you something's going wrong in his head."

"Stop calling me little brother. I was born three seconds after you, for Pete's sake. Also, I don't buy he's lost it. If you were out of control, you would surely seem like you're out of control?"

"Did you see what he did to that fucker, Walker, from the Nucleus?" Scott asked.

"I saw. The boss barely broke a sweat, never once raised his voice."

"Precisely. Doesn't that worry you?"

Brad sighed and evaded two potholes. "His wife left him. Got to forgive a man some frayed edges."

"She came back."

Brad took his eyes off the road for a moment to look at his brother. "Really?"

Scott nodded. "Tail between her legs."

"Shit," Brad said, looking back at the road. "You really do have his ear."

"I did. Not sure I do anymore. He just keeps emphasising that he's got it all under control. That's all I get these days."

"He killed that woman on the steps of the station. I guess that's got to have an impact?"

"I agree. That was the start, no question. Something just woke up in him."

"An epiphany! Where the hell did Margaret see this rig anyways?"

"On this road, little brother. Keep on, we'll get there."

"Fuck you with the little brother. Anyway, let's agree the boss just needs time, then. His wife's home, and the shock of killing that bitch from the core will wear off. You always get so goddamned worried about him."

"Because he's been like a father to me."

"We have a father."

Scott snorted.

"Of sorts," Brad said. "Try not to get too worried. I just wish he'd hurry up and crack Walker."

"And then what, little ... sorry ... brother? Guns drawn, we hit the Nucleus like the OK Corral?"

Brad smiled. "Now you're speaking my language. Shit ... there it is." He pulled the police cruiser to a halt behind the rig. He confirmed the licence plate with the one that

Margaret had called into the station. "Yep, it's him alright. Everyone's favorite praying mantis, Logan Reed."

* * *

Interrupted from his book again, Albert had to supress his irritation from a potential customer. However, his decorum was short lived when he saw who was in his shop. The woman, who wore the usual cotton attire of the Nucleus's people, along with a beanie hat, prowled his magazine stand.

He gritted his teeth but carefully contemplated his words. He wasn't about to make the same quip he'd used on Gordon about ruining his magazine stand with blood, chiefly because he wanted no interaction whatsoever. She was from the rotten core, and he wanted her off his property immediately.

"I think you've come to the wrong store, lady."

"I don't think so, Albert."

He wasn't too fazed she knew his name; it was written on his door, after all. "I won't ask nicely again."

She didn't look at him and, instead, reached down for a magazine. "You didn't ask nicely the first time."

"There's a reason for that."

"Go on." She flicked through the magazine.

"Your people are a vile lot."

She returned the magazine to the stand. "I couldn't agree more."

Albert creased his brow. He wasn't in the mood for a back and forth with a peculiar woman from that accursed place. He reached under the counter and placed a hand on his shotgun. "Take it up with your kin. Irrelevant to me if our views are the same. I want you out."

She turned, and he, despite the beanie covering her hair, recognized her. He'd seen her skulking around Brady Crossing before.

"You've a right to hate the Nucleus, Albert. They took something from you."

Her words seized him. As one of his hands was already on the shotgun, he used his other hand to steady himself against the counter. "I don't know who you are, but ... but—"

"Those people, my people, took the only thing you've ever cared about."

"Who are you?"

She took several steps forward and slipped off her beanie. She was completely bald. Maybe he'd been mistaken after all; he didn't recall ever seeing a bald female from the Nucleus before. "Are you reaching for your gun, Albert? Killing me would leave you with a lot of curiosity."

"I ... I ..." He shook his head. *Get control of yourself, dammit!*

"You loved her, didn't you?"

He shook his head. "These're things you can't possibly know about."

"Roseleigh?"

The name felt like a cold hand clutching at him.

She took another couple of steps forward. He slipped his fingers around the shotgun.

"Have you forgotten her? She never forgot about you. I promise you that."

He shook his head. "Is she ...?"

"Yes, I'm afraid. A long time ago now."

He flinched. Tears sprang up in his eyes. "How?"

"The usual way. Illness. Sadness. *Loneliness*. She had a

47

life, but I never think she got over you—her coalminer from the Crossing."

He rubbed at his eyes, cleared the tears, and saw that the gaunt, bald woman was now at his counter. "It was my fault. I should have known better. I knew where she was from. I put her in danger. Did she ever have children? She always wanted children."

The woman smiled. "Only one. She used to keep something to remind her of you that her husband, who has also passed, never knew about. But her child knew."

Suspecting that this was Roseleigh's child, he lifted his hand from the shotgun. "What was it she kept?"

"Your palm?"

He offered it to her.

"My name is Corrie." She placed a lump of coal into his hand and closed his hand into a fist around it.

"Are you her daughter?"

Corrie nodded. "But that isn't everything."

Realizing he was now crying more freely, he rubbed at his tears again. "What do you mean?"

"The Nucleus didn't just take Roseleigh from you. Look at my eyes."

He looked at the coal in his hand and cupped her face with the other—one green eye, one blue. *Just like his.*

"They took your daughter too."

* * *

Expecting to find Logan either asleep or dead from a heart attack, the two brothers, Brad and Scott, didn't approach the rig with too much caution. However, when it became clear that Logan was not in the cab or the storage container, the adrenaline kicked in, and they drew their weapons.

Brad circled the vehicle and reported back to Scott. "No flat tires."

Scott holstered his weapon, hopped into the cab, and, seeing the keys hanging from the ignition, fired up the engine. The gauge showed a healthy level of fuel.

"He didn't break down, then!" Scott shouted down.

"So, why did he abandon his vehicle?"

Your guess is as good as mine, brother.

Scott exited down to the road and unholstered his weapon again. Together, they walked to the roadside. There was a sharp hillside, which led down into a patch of bushes. "Fancy a look?" Scott asked.

"He's probably just wandered back into town."

Scott shook his head. "Nah. It's a long walk, and so rather pointless if your truck hasn't broken down."

"The bushes it is, I guess."

They headed down to check the hillside bushes. Apart from a couple of rusted old tins, some used prophylactics, and the remains of a dead animal, there was no sign of the missing truck driver.

"Shit, a missing out-of-towner," Scott said. "That's all the boss needs."

4

That evening, Gordon ditched the coffee and drank the whiskey neat from his 'I Love New York' mug.

"You remember Delmonico's, Susan?" he called to her in the bedroom. "Lobster Newburg. You went nuts for it." As he drank from the mug, he watched, with pride, the stillness of his hand. The trembling was gone. Just like this broken mug, he'd mended his life.

"A lifetime ago," she replied. "Back before you became so *fucking* serious."

The whiskey stung his throat and burned his gut. "Life gets serious for everyone."

"Maybe, but not everyone gets so goddamned boring!"

"Nothing changes, does it? You were always so pissed at—"

"Pissed, you fat fuck? *Pissed?* Understatement of the year! You fucking killed me!"

"One way of looking at it."

"Other ways? There's a bullet in my brain! What *other ways* are there?"

"I froze time, Susan." He drank the remains of his

whiskey, sighed, closed his eyes, and leaned back on the chair. "I stopped you from destroying everything we built together. I stopped you from embarrassing yourself, embarrassing me. Everything can just, you know, remain."

"You stupid man. You and your status quo, keeping everything the same. Is it any wonder you get no respect? That you're a laughingstock? You let the Nucleus thrive, and now everyone looks at you with disdain."

He took a deep breath, still feeling remarkably calm, despite his wife's taunts. "I'm not letting you take me down with you. I've never felt more ... more ... what's the word? *Goddammit* ... purposeful. That's it!"

She guffawed. "You think people will follow you into that rotten place?"

"Scott will. Brad will."

"They look at you like a father; what does that say about them?"

"They're good boys."

"They're pathetic imbeciles!"

He rose to his feet and rolled his shoulders. "There'll be others."

"Like the shopkeeper, Albert Hardy? How much support did he offer you today?"

"He'll come around."

"Because you're so *fucking* persuasive, aren't you?"

He grabbed his mug and held it at arm's length—again, admiring the steadiness of his nerves. "You can't get to me anymore, Susan."

"Because I'm dead, you weasel! It's a little bit of an extreme measure to put your mind at ease!"

"It was my only choice. I needed the peace."

"Poor choice! You're still talking to me!"

He wandered into the kitchen, picked up a bottle of Old Crow, and refilled his mug. "I find it stimulating."

"And when you're fucking my cold, stiff body, do you find that stimulating too?"

He took another swig and grunted. "Always so coarse, Susan. You always did enjoy debasing my feelings for you—"

His cellphone rang, interrupting the conversation. He saw that it was Scott. "Okay, son?"

"Exhausted. We've rattled the cage in Mossbark. No luck, whatsoever, boss. Nobody has seen or heard from Logan Reed. He hasn't headed back. You think he stopped for a piss and a bear took him or something?"

Gordon laughed. "That's not happened around here, at least not in my lifetime. We have black bears—rather small and docile. I don't think it will be that. Neither do we have venomous snakes before you raise that option. Besides, you searched the bushes, right?"

"Yes, boss. Thoroughly."

"The man wasn't of sound mind really, was he?" He could hear Susan laughing in the other room.

"I don't really know—"

"Well, anyone who gets involved with Frank Yorke and the Nucleus is not of sound mind, are they? Also, the man wanders in and out of this town like it's his playground. Who does that?"

"I did hear that Cindy, the woman he was seeing, went back to her husband."

"There you have it! He was depressed. I bet he wandered off into the middle of nowhere, suicidal."

He heard Susan laughing again. "Police work at its finest!"

Instinctively, Gordon cupped the cellphone so Scott

wouldn't hear her, despite knowing this was an impossibility. He thought for a moment, then lifted his hand away again. "Have the rig towed to our compound in Sharp Point."

"And file a missing person's report?"

"Yes, but include the report that he was seen wandering off into the outback alone."

"A report, from who?"

"Anonymous. Or find someone? I can't do everything for you, Scott."

"Why a report?"

"Because eventually, someone is going to miss this suicidal drifter, so they need a suitable narrative for his disappearance. Do you want to investigate a possible crime? Do you care about this man that much?"

"I guess not."

"So, let's not attract the attention of the MSP. You remember the fish we are currently frying?"

"Yes."

"Precisely."

"But, sir?"

"Yes, son?"

"What if he's in danger? What if someone took him?"

Gordon chortled. "Who? What could anyone possibly want with that man?"

"The Nucleus. They have been known to take people before, after all."

"He's a friend of the goddamned Nucleus! You know who is currently living up there, don't you? Frank Yorke. Those two are as thick as thieves!"

"I guess you're right, Sheriff."

"Of course, I am! So, keep the noise over this down, okay?"

"I will. Oh … and, boss?"

"Yes."

"Leo's back again."

"Again? *Jesus.* We only let him out four hours back!"

"It seems it only took him four hours to get blind drunk again. Except, this time, he came to us of his accord. Marched into the station and shouted obscenities at me. So I threw him in the can."

"He played you like a fiddle, Scott. He was after a warm bed."

"I'll turn off the heat!" Scott said and laughed.

"Don't do that. I don't want you freezing our other guest to death."

"Fair point."

"Goodnight, son."

"Goodnight, boss."

Gordon finished the whiskey and headed to the office. As he passed the open bedroom door, the odor of his dead wife intensified. "Jesus."

"Your fault, Gordon."

"Small price to pay for peace of mind."

"Peace of mind!" She laughed again. "How long will your peace of mind last when you are brushing missing persons' cases under the carpet?"

"Long enough to do what needs to be done." He closed the bedroom door and kicked the draft excluder into place. Then he headed into the office, where he studied the aerial images of the Nucleus. He stepped forward and pressed his finger to the northernmost forest. "Tomorrow."

"Tomorrow, what?" Susan asked.

"Tomorrow, I'm going into the rotten core with or without Walker."

"Suicide!"

"Maybe, but I'm through waiting."

"And what do you expect to do if, and when, you get there?"

"I don't know yet. One step at a time. I just want to know if I can get to them; whether or not the war begins tomorrow, I cannot say."

"You've failed at everything in your life, Gordon. You'll fail at that too."

"You always had such faith in me, Susan. It's a shame you're dead."

"It'll be a shame for you when someone finds out."

* * *

Jake drank a glass of water, wishing it was beer, but his own store of that had run dry, and no one from the Nucleus was doing a town run until the weekend. He could make the journey himself, but the prospect of leaving Celestia to the mercy of the more untrustworthy members of the Nucleus, as well as those who could now gain access through the southernmost forest, made his mouth run dry—dry enough for him to have to get up and refill his glass.

"Cards?" Celestia asked from her bedroom door.

"You planning to hustle me?" Jake turned and leaned against the kitchen wall.

"No, just bored, and the quiet is bothering me."

"It's quiet like a church. Name the film?"

"Easy. *The Hustler*. 'Fast Eddie' Felson. Quiet like a church. Church of the Good Hustler."

Jake laughed. "It looks more like a morgue to me." He pointed to the table. "Those tables are the slabs they lay the stiffs on."

Celestia nodded; her eyes were full of admiration. "I'll be alive when I get out, Charlie."

I hope so, Jake thought. *I really do hope so.* "Let's play."

They played Texas hold'em poker, using matchsticks. They bounced around a few more quotations from their favorite movies, and Jake felt the urge for a beer to slip away. More importantly, he felt the weight of anxiety shifting slightly. He couldn't ignore the fact that danger was pressing in on Celestia from all sides, but at least his reason for being here was suddenly clear again: friendship. And as Jake well knew, friendship in this strange and twisted world could never be underestimated.

After a few hands of poker, Jake put down his cards. "I'm beat. And not just at cards. I mean tired."

Celestia put down her cards and glanced at her chewed nails. "Remember all the grief you gave me about my nails when we first met?"

"For good reason. They were deadly weapons."

She raised her hands and wriggled them. "All gone. You see, I *listened* to you. I *trusted* you."

"The world's a safer—"

"Why don't you *listen* to me, Jake? Why don't you *trust* me?" She looked him in the eyes.

"I'm so proud of you, Celestia."

"Pride isn't trust, Jake."

"I know." He sighed. "Look, it's late. We need to be fresh tomorrow, so we should—"

"Why do we need to be fresh tomorrow?"

Because we have no idea what is coming, or when it's coming. "It's just a good idea. These are strange times."

"Cut the bullshit. I need you. You know that. But I cannot carry on like this. We're either a team or we aren't!"

Jake shook his head and sighed.

"What?"

"Team? I'll give you your definition of a team. Recognize this quotation: it's a very difficult job, and the only way to get through it is if we all work together as a team. And that means you do everything I say."

She narrowed her eyes. "Charlie Croker. *The Italian Job*. It's bullshit, Jake. We talk, and I listen."

"Do you?"

"Yes, but there is no point in me leading this place if I don't do what I believe in. You need to be more supportive of that."

"I cannot be supportive of anything that might get you killed—"

A knock sounded at the door.

Celestia rose, but Jake was on his feet and at the door quicker.

"My hero," she hissed as he opened it.

It was Everlyn, mother of two and leader of the Nucleus's soldiers. Even though she had aided the late Griffin during his uprising on the Great Day of Burning when he had mercilessly slaughtered Merithew, Celestia trusted her. Not that she had any choice. Nearly all the Nucleus's soldiers had aided Griffin that day.

"It's late," Jake said.

"I know," Everlyn said. "It's important."

Jake narrowed his eyes, then regarded Celestia.

The young leader nodded.

"Lift up your arms," Jake said, preparing to search.

"I have a gun. And a knife," Everlyn said. "I *always* have a gun and a knife."

"Leave it," Celestia said, stepping forward. "If anybody wanted me dead, they've had plenty of opportunities already. Come in, Everlyn."

Jake stepped backward and crossed his arms. "Fine, but I'm not going anywhere."

Celestia's shrug said it all. *Suit yourself.*

Everlyn sat at the table with Jake and Celestia. "I've not got a great deal to say."

"Anything you have to say," Celestia said, "you can say here, and you'll be listened to. Things are different now."

Celestia sat upright, and despite her very youthful face, she did convey herself in a statesmanlike way. Jake had been telling her the truth before. He *was* proud of her. She'd stepped up to the task without hesitation and was not anything but dogged and determined.

But he couldn't deny her naivety. Celestia was wide open here to people who weren't naïve, and certainly not innocent. Jake knew it was only a matter of time before he had to firmly intervene or walk away. Both options could have deadly consequences.

"I don't have too much to say," Everlyn said.

Why would she? She was an example of the people Celestia should be fearing—the worldly wise, those who could keep their cards firmly to their chests.

"I speak on behalf of several of us, Celestia," Everlyn said.

"Who?"

"Fern, Ibre, and Glynnie."

Three more of the late Griffin's closest soldiers.

It's happening. Right in front of me, where I sit. It's fucking happening.

"Thaxton?" Celestia asked.

Everlyn said, "No, just us four."

But most of your goddamned army, Celestia!

"And what would you like to bring to my attention?"

"The disarming. We are struggling to make good with this."

Jake looked down at the table, supressing a sigh.

"Why?" Celestia asked.

"Because we have children. We have a community to protect."

"But, Everlyn, you yourself more than anyone saw what my father and his successor, Griffin, brought to the Nucleus. Have you forgotten the suffering?"

"I think you overestimate the suffering. Our world was calm."

"The world may have seemed calm to you, but it wasn't to the people my father brought here to be raped and killed. And it wasn't for the children of these victims that Griffin rounded up and tried to kill—"

"We accept that there was turbulence, but the greater picture always requires some turbulence."

"Does it?" Celestia raised an eyebrow. "Does it *really?* Must people die in order that you may live?"

Everlyn sat back in her chair. "That's not what I mean. We've stood in the square with you, we have sat in our internal meetings with you, we accepted the demise of the elders. So far, we have embraced your desire to change. But this is a bridge too far. You are welcoming our enemies onto us."

"It's not true. Why can't we believe in the goodness of Mossbark? Why can't we extend our hand to them?"

"Because they're part of the world—the world your ancestor, Althea, rejected."

"And I say, you must not lose faith in humanity. Humanity is like an ocean; if a few drops of the ocean are dirty, the ocean does not become dirty."

Ghandi. You really have taken the time to educate yourself, haven't you, Celestia?

"I never had any faith in humanity," Everlyn said.

"Yes. And that is our mistake. We need to start."

"And is that your answer, Celestia?"

"My answer?"

"Your answer to our request to halt the disarming?"

"I'm sorry. I do not hear that request. I can understand why you made it, but I cannot hear it. I love you, Fern, Ibre, and Glynnie too much to hear it. You've trusted me as your leader, and now I must finish what I have started. The old ways didn't work."

"The old ways kept our children safe. How do you want me to word your response to the others?"

"The same way I have worded it to you, Everlyn. Tell them I love them, that I believe the world, *our* world, can be and will be how it was meant to be."

Everlyn rose.

Jake felt like burying his head in his hands but, instead, looked up at her. He retained a stoic expression. He had to present himself as strong, despite feeling himself crumbling inside.

"And you, Frank Yorke, being one of those outside, what do you think lies in store for us?" Everlyn asked.

He exchanged a look with Celestia, who, for the first time since Everlyn arrived, appeared unsettled. He faced Everlyn. "I think you'll have to trust your leader. I know I do."

5

ollowing an impromptu visit from an estranged daughter, Albert had returned home to his drinks' cabinet, and his memory of Roseleigh. In these, his elderly years, many of his memories lacked clarity, but not this one. *Never this one.*

Beautiful, soft-skinned Roseleigh ... what had she been doing that night in The Oak? Smiling across a crowded room of drunken, tired miners at young Albert Hardy. Local rebel. The boy who'd told his father to stick the convenience store—the family business—where the sun doesn't shine. He was going down into the pits with the boys he'd grown up with.

"Roseleigh," Albert sighed, lying back on his bed, drunk on wine. "Roseleigh, why did you choose me?" He folded his arms and rolled onto his side.

He didn't even have a photograph to call on. Roseleigh had never allowed it. It was forbidden in the world she came from. And it wouldn't pay for her to keep evidence of her weekly excursions into Brady County.

Not that he needed a photograph to recall that wild black hair that she refused to ever cut, nor did he need one to remember the dimples in her cheeks he would run the end of his nose, and sometimes his tongue, over time and time again.

"Why *choose* me?" Albert asked.

But *why* was irrelevant. The only relevance was that she *had*.

In The Oak, his nails and hair blackened with coal, he'd danced with her, when Jeremy, an Irish immigrant, played his guitar and crooned. From out of town, Roseleigh had claimed; visiting relatives in Sharp Point, she had assured him. Every week, she'd returned. And on every one of those nights, they'd danced.

"And I fell in love with you," Albert said.

And she'd fallen in love with him. At least she'd told him so, often after they'd made love in a motel room, and then, more than three times a week.

"But I should have asked. I should have asked so much sooner than I did. Where're you from? *Really?*"

Always nine o'clock. Never ten o'clock. Never even five-past. Nine was the time she'd leave him to return to Sharp Point.

"Except, you'd lied," Albert said.

One night, he'd followed her up the hill into the woods to a place where no one dared go—the Nucleus.

Even now, lying in bed, he cried again over the realization she'd been from a forbidden world. He'd loved her passionately, *sexually*, so many times, yet the truth threatened everything.

Seized by desire and desperation to keep her, it had taken every ounce of his willpower to stop himself from going back into the heart of that evil place that fateful night.

And he knew now that if he had done, then he wouldn't be here now.

"For all my life had been worth since that moment I lost you."

For days after she'd disappeared into the Nucleus, he endured loss of the worse possible kind. It felt like the person he loved with every ounce of his being was dead. When she didn't return the following week, he'd assumed that those from that accursed place now knew about him and all her freedoms had been stripped away.

"If you'd ever actually loved me in the first place."

A week had passed before he'd returned to that place on the hill. He had looked into the darkness that was forbidden to the world of men. Someone had peered back at him from the gloom, and his heart had missed a beat. *Is it her? Peering at me from behind the trees?* He had thought, but his answer had come in the form of a bullet, which snapped past him, caused a shower of bark, and sent him fleeing for his life.

The following day, his father had summoned him from the mine to the convenience store. They hadn't spoken for months. A broken young man, Albert lacked the energy to continue his rebellion though and had answered his father's call, immediately. It had been a trap.

Two tall men dressed in flimsy cotton garments had welcomed him into the store. "Filthy looking men." Not filthy in the same way that he and his friends were. There was no coal etched into their skin and dusting their hair. Filthy in the disgust they made him feel as they had skulked around the shop floor, sneering.

He'd known who they were and where they were from.

He'd apologized to his father, who cowered behind a counter, staring into the barrel of his own shotgun, which one of these filthy, cold intruders must have plucked from his aging hands. He had then asked them, bluntly, whether they meant to kill him or his father.

"I didn't mind dying so much at that point, way I was feeling, Roseleigh, but that stubborn old mule didn't deserve this."

But the only thing that died that day had been Albert's heart when he vowed to forget Roseleigh and never again venture up that hill to that dark place in the woods.

Appeased, the men had left.

"Left me to my future, Roseleigh." Albert rolled onto his side. "Working alongside my father until his death, before finally becoming the proprietor of Hardy's conveniences. Alone. But content. Having nothing to do with your world. Your people. Until. Yes, until. Her eyes are two different colors, just like mine. And her nose, dare I say it, long and bony, like my own. I'm an old man, Roseleigh. The final finishing line is in sight. And you've just changed everything. Again. Just like you did all those years ago."

He fell asleep, remembering Corrie's final words to him on this day of great change.

I need your help, Father. Myself and your grandson, Marston, need your help.

* * *

"Albert listened." Corrie stood behind Marston, who was sitting at the kitchen table, drawing. "He listened, and I think he understood." She ran her fingers through her boy's hair. "I may have doubted it myself if not for those eyes. And, of course, for how much you look like him, Marston."

Marston, who had said very little since murdering his adopted sister, remained silent as he drew.

She leaned over his shoulder and saw that he was sketching a picture of someone lying on the floor. "You always had talent. I always had such high hopes for you. I'm sorry this place destroyed your life."

She watched her son's hand move quickly as he added definition to the figure's face. It soon became clear that the person lying on the floor was male.

"Merithew always kept our ties to the communities below us strong. It was what kept us safe."

Marston was now sketching a second figure standing beside the lying man.

"His ties to Gordon Kane in the Mossbark Police Department. The money he provided to the storeowners. It was an ecosystem, Marston—a safely functioning ecosystem. With that gone, our entire world is vulnerable."

It was already becoming clear that the second figure was a woman.

"But we have something now. We have Albert. He's a start, a new connection. I have asked him to meet us tomorrow, and I believe he will ... You're so fast, Marston. How fast does your mind move for you to sketch so quickly?" She noticed Marston was not adding hair to the female. "Is that me, Marston?"

He gave a slight nod.

She could distinguish the movement because she had her hand in his hair.

He then drew something in her hand.

She watched the shape evolve. Her blood ran cold. "Why are you drawing me with a knife, Marston?"

He didn't answer. Instead, he grabbed a red crayon and scribbled over the prone man on the floor. Eventually, he pushed the crayon down so hard that the wax crumbled. He grunted as he worked, desperate to completely conceal the dead man in red. When he finished, he let the crayon fall to the table. He then rubbed at the red splodge. "My father."

She stepped backward, her body threatening to shatter into a thousand pieces.

6

With whiskey-laced coffee in hand, Sheriff Gordon Kane arrived at his department to find Scott pacing outside his office.

"One of those nights, eh? Used to hate the late shift." Gordon thrust his key into the office door. "One day, when you have this office, son, you won't have to do them anymore."

"I fucked up ..."

Gordon held his office door open for Scott and gestured him inside. "Okay, son. Nothing in relation to that little problem regarding the dog with two dicks, Logan Reed, I hope?"

Scott didn't go into the office. "No. I did exactly what you said, boss. His rig is now up at Sharp Point, and my good friend, Dom, saw him wandering off into the unknown, blind drunk."

Gordon winked at him. "Good. So, why the ants in the pants, son? Come in."

"I think you better come and have a look, Sheriff. I *really* fucked up."

Gordon sighed, closed his office door, and locked it again. "Lead the way, son."

* * *

"Leo, Leo, Leo ..." Gordon muttered to himself as he checked the town drunk's pulse. *Nothing. And freezing cold to boot. See you later, alligator.* He exited the cell and found Scott at the entrance to the cellblock.

"Did I fuck up?"

Gordon smiled. "Only in so much as you didn't clean up the spew he choked on. Stinks to high heaven in there."

"Yes, but he's dead, isn't he?"

"As a doornail. Who'd you tell?"

"No one. I tried calling you, but you didn't answer."

"For good reason. I was asleep. But I don't mean who did you announce his passing to; I mean, who knows he's here?"

"Apart from you, no one. Walker obviously knows he's in an adjacent cell again, but they don't communicate, so he won't know he's dead."

"Did you log him in?"

Scott shook his head. "Sorry, boss. I'll do it—"

"No, that's fine, son. You say he came into the department of his own accord, last night?"

Scott nodded.

"So, to conclude, we are absolutely certain no one knows he's here?"

"Unless he told someone he was coming here, I guess. But he has no friends or family, and most people just tend to ignore him anyway—unless they are serving him alcohol in the liquor store."

Gordon thought for a moment. "Lock down the station for an hour."

"Why, sir?"

"Just do it. And let Brad and Riley know they can come in late today."

"Won't they wonder why?"

"Yes, but I'm sure they won't mind much when they are eating their doughnuts, aren't you? Go and contact them, son."

"Okay, and then what?"

"Come back to the cells, and this is what I want you to do."

Gordon unlocked Walker's cell door and slid it all the way across. Then he filled the gap with his portly frame and outstretched his arms so one hand was gripping a metal bar on the cell door and the other was pressed against the brick frame.

With his back to Gordon, Walker lay on his stripped concrete bunk.

"Do you mind, pussy? I'm sleeping," Walker said.

"With no mattress?" Gordon asked.

"I can sleep anywhere. Especially here. Not like I need to sleep with one eye open, is it? There're bars between me and the world."

"You slept? Really? With all those fucking bruises?"

Walker flipped over. With swollen eyes, he peered at Gordon through a gap in his long, blood-stained hair. "You call that a beating? Ha! You've no idea. One day, I'll show you a real beating."

"Let's be realistic here, Walker. That's an opportunity that will never arise."

"What do you want, pussy?"

"To present you with that one chance again." He took his hand from the brick and held up a finger. "The one chance I've been presenting to you for quite a length of time now. You recall that I have warned you, time and time again, about the expiry date?"

"The expiry date that never comes!"

Gordon nodded and grinned. "Well, guess what? It's come."

Walker sat upright on his bunk and swung his legs off so he was opposite Gordon. He glared at him, before bursting into laughter, stopping, and wincing when he'd antagonized his injuries for an impressive number of seconds. "We've a saying in the Nucleus, Sheriff. Nothing catches a flapping fish better than bare hands. Do you know what it means?"

"No, I can't say I do, or that I'm interested."

"Think about it. How many times do you think someone from the Nucleus has been forced to catch a flapping fish?"

"Not too many? I don't think there are many rivers up where you are."

"Many times, Gordon." Walker cracked his neck. "Many, many times. Always, we have faced these flapping fish, but always"—he clapped his hands together—"we catch them, use them, eat them if necessary. Because nothing catches a flapping fish better than bare hands."

"I'm sure. I wouldn't have the patience, personally. I prefer the rod—"

"You know our joke regarding you, Sheriff?"

"No ... is it funny?"

Walker smiled and stood. "The joke is that of all the fish we caught, Sheriff Gordon Kane, you were the one fish who didn't flap. You were still. *Dead* still. The easiest catch we ever made."

Gordon narrowed his eyes. "I've a saying too."

"Do you now?"

"Never trust the quiet ones. They're good at playing dead."

Walker smiled. "Don't worry. We never trusted you, Sheriff. We were just surprised by how easy you made it for us." He stepped forward.

"Stop there."

Walker took a second step.

Scott came up alongside Gordon, unholstering his gun.

Walker shrugged and went to sit back on the bunk. "When do I get to see my lawyer?"

"You don't," Gordon said. "No one knows you're here. In fact, no one even found out what happened to Angelita. We buried her far from here. It's where we will bury you, today, if you decide to let my offer expire."

Walker sneered. "I respect that you're trying to flap now, little fishy, but I just don't buy it."

Gordon turned to Scott. "Is the station locked?"

Scott nodded.

"Good." Gordon turned to face Walker.

"You want me to deal with Leo first?" Scott asked.

"No, I'll do it, son. Nothing will give me greater pleasure than to flap for this motherfucker, before we send him to kingdom come."

Walker chuckled, shaking his head. "Bullshit."

"Keep your gun on him, Scott, but keep that finger steady. I know how it twitches. I don't want to have to get rid of your gun unless I must. Just gets messy."

Walker clapped. "What a performance."

Gordon stepped backward, while Scott edged farther into the cell.

"He's the best shot in town, Walker. I wouldn't even raise an eyebrow. On your right eye, that is. Your left eye looks fucked to hell."

Walker clapped again.

Gordon smiled and entered the adjacent cell, which was standing open. Unlike Walker, Leo had been provided with a mattress. Gordon approached the corpse. "I'm sorry, Leo. I just can't risk it, the things you may have overheard." He leaned in to grab the pillow behind the dead man's head and winced over the smell of vomit that assaulted his nostrils and the back of his throat. He raised his voice. "It'll be easier than I thought, Scott. The bastard's dead to the world."

"The only thing that'll happen to that poor bastard," Walker shouted, "is he'll wake up with a sore ass!"

Gordon smiled. He felt a sudden surge of adrenaline. He couldn't remember the last time he'd felt so alive. He pressed the pillow over dead Leo's face to try to block the rising stench of sick. "Shit, he's waking." Gordon grunted dramatically as he pretended to wrestle with a waking man.

"Hope he kicks your ass!" Walker shouted.

Continuing to feign a struggle, Gordon pondered what he was about to do and was glad Leo had no family or real friends in Mossbark—not because they'd come looking for him but rather because they would have to behold the man's remains *afterward*.

Gordon threw the pillow to one side, stood back, and bit deep into his own wrist. Pain tore through him, and even after his mouth filled with blood, he bit deeper. Eventually, when he really could stand no more, he yanked his head away and roared in agony. "Get off me, you *fucker!*" He slammed his fist into Leo's face.

"What's going on in there?" Scott called from the other cell.

"He bit me. He *fucking* bit me." He hit the dead man again, feeling his nose explode against his fist.

"Sheriff, are you all right? I'm coming—"

"*No!* I've got it under control." He surveyed the state of his arm. He'd done a fine job on himself. He could barely see the teeth marks for all the blood. "Look what you've done to me, you sonofabitch." He leaned over and punched Leo in the face again. "Look, what you've done!" Each time he hit him, he shouted louder. He wanted to sound like a desperate man on the edge.

He ran out the cell and back to the other one. He stared in to see Scott a foot from Walker with his gun pointed down at his head. "Look what the fucker did!" He waved his injured arm in the air. "Look at it."

Scott chanced a quick glance backward. "Sheriff, are you okay?"

Walker smiled. "Serves you right—"

Gordon roared. He shook the bars of the cell. He made himself look like a man possessed. "I'm going to tear his fucking head off!"

He ran back into the other cell. He grabbed Leo's hair and yanked him from his bunk. The corpse hit the floor with a loud thump. "No one will fucking recognize you."

Flapping fish! I'll give you flapping fish, Walker.

He leaned down and hooked his arms under the corpse's armpits and dragged him across the cell floor. "Look at my goddamned arm, you bastard."

He slid him alongside Walker's open cell door, and just before the brick wall, he turned inward. He had his back to

Walker, but he knew Scott still had Walker at gunpoint. There was no danger.

He dropped Leo so his head rested at the entrance to the cell by the brick wall, exactly opposite from the sliding door.

Gordon made a real show of it. He turned to the wall himself and pounded his fists against it. "I bet you've given me AIDS. You fucker! You bit right to the fucking bone!" He kicked the wall and howled. He turned back to the corpse and prodded his face with his boot. "Wake up! I want you to feel every bit of this." He kicked his head harder. "Wake up!"

"The man isn't waking up," Walker said behind him. "He's out like a light. You need to get control—"

"I'll show you control, you Nucleus slug." He grabbed the cell door and yanked. It slid over the freshly oiled runners. There was a whoosh, followed by a sickening crunch. "It's time people woke up"—Gordon wheeled the cell door open again, forcing himself to look down at Leo's now misshapen head—"to how serious things have gotten around here."

Whoosh. Crunch.

Again, he forced himself to look, and this time felt extreme revulsion.

One of Leo's eyes was protruding.

"You brought this on yourself."

Whoosh. Crunch. Whoosh. Crunch.

Leo's head had folded in on itself.

It was too disgusting; Gordon closed his eyes and drove the cell door back and forth until it eventually connected with the frame, and the latch engaged with the strike plate. He turned, opening his eyes to glimpse Scott first, who was pale and trembling; he'd even lowered his weapon, which was dangerous.

Not that it mattered. Walker had scurried to the top of his bunk and was squashed into the corner. His eyes were wide, and his mouth hung open slightly.

Gordon darted forward and snatched the gun from Scott's hand.

Scott scurried backward to the other corner of the cell, crossing his arms over his face. He wasn't acting. Despite knowing it was a performance, his young mind had succumbed to the horror.

Gordon stepped forward, pointing the gun at Walker's head. "Time up, Walker. Call me a fish? Pick an eye, or I'll pick for you, you fucking slug. Three seconds to point one out. One ..." He cocked the gun. "Two ... Three—"

"Okay ... okay!" Walker said, also with his arms crossed over his face now. "I'll tell you. I'll tell you how to get in."

*"*You won't just tell me, slug. You'll fucking show me."

7

J ake found Celestia beside the charred remains of Pastor Banks' church.

"I hope you're not paying your respects to that bastard. He was anything but a man of God."

"Of course not. That monster, this church were some of the things that changed my father for the worst. The reason I'm here, Jake, is because someone very special died here."

"The elder? Gillie?"

Celestia nodded.

"She must have been special to you, then. I've seen what you did to her colleagues."

Celestia glowered at him. "They made their choices. Gillie would never have sat and listened to the bile Lynna was spouting."

"She might have been too old to deliver three clear head-shots though."

Celestia shrugged. "I'm doing all of this for her. If it wasn't for Gillie, if it wasn't for what she taught me to be, I wouldn't have it in me to stay and fight for what's right."

"It's her fault, then?"

Celestia sighed.

Jake nodded toward a group of people in the square. "The problem is that Everlyn and her companions don't think you've got any fight in you."

Celestia nodded. "Do you know they've been standing there, in discussion, since I sent Thaxton to disarm the northernmost forest?"

"Alone?"

Celestia nodded again, slowly this time. "None of the others would go."

Jake's blood ran cold.

She turned to face him. "Merithew and Griffin's soldiers are not playing follow the leader anymore."

"Celestia—"

"Don't, Jake. Don't tell me you told me so."

*"That's not what I was going to say."

*"Oh really?"

Jake turned from her, his heart thrashing in his chest. He bit his thumbnail. It was over.

*"Gillie taught me how important it was to fight without violence," Celestia said. "She told me the stories; she was always the voice of reason on that council. She wasn't there when they voted to execute my father. She never would have accepted that, which is why they did it in her absence."

*"Would she have accepted what you did to the council?"

*"No, of course not, but what choice did I have?"

*"Well, we're out of choices now. We must leave," Jake said, turning back.

*"No. I'm going to finish what I've started."

*"How? You said yourself they're not supporting you anymore."

*"They aren't. But others in the Nucleus believe in me."

"Yes, but these soldiers are the dangerous ones, not the children and farmers in the Focus!"

Celestia shrugged.

"You can't just keep killing people who refuse to do what you say. That makes you a tyrant, and I'm pretty sure that would have Gillie doing somersaults in her grave."

"I'm not killing anyone else. Everlyn and the others are simply refusing to disarm the Nucleus, so we shall do it. No harm will come to them if they don't rise against me. I want them to see what we can achieve. Tomorrow, once we're disarmed, I'll head into Brady Crossing to make peace with Mossbark County, and everyone will see what is possible."

Jake eyed the small gathering in the square. He didn't need to be a fly on the wall to know what they were talking about. For Celestia, time was running out. If she was going to make her outlandish plan work, which he severely doubted she would, she'd better hurry up.

"I'm going to help Thaxton," Celestia said. "Are you coming?"

Jake nodded. "Why not? Always wanted to disarm beartraps."

Albert walked the dirt track which led to the disused mine, wondering if the events of the previous day had been real or the delusion of an aging mind. Had a woman from the Nucleus really walked into his store to tell him that he was her father?

When he turned from the dirt path to face the mine entrance that tunneled into the mountainside, he saw Corrie standing on the steel track beside an overturned cart.

Behind her was a boy, turned away from him, with his hands on the iron door that sealed off the disused pit.

It had been real. His heart thrashed in his chest, and he feared it may just give in right now and rob him of this chance to fully understand the mystery of his life.

He drew closer.

"Father," Corrie said.

He flinched. The word didn't feel right. He wondered if it ever would. "Corrie." He nodded at the boy with his hands on the iron door. "Is this ...?"

"Your grandson. Marston."

A breath left Albert's lungs, and he struggled to draw it back in. He stepped forward so he was alongside his daughter. He felt her hand on the small of his back. He stared at the boy several yards ahead of him.

Up close, Albert could see that the iron door had come loose from its top hinges. It had started to fall inward but had stayed upright, after catching a low-hanging wooden beam, which itself must also have come loose from supporting the roof. It would be easy for someone to slip through the gap afforded by the tilting door. He wondered if Marston was considering that now and shuddered. No good could come from going into that ancient tomb.

"Marston?" Albert said.

The boy didn't turn.

"Marston, turn and meet your grandfather," Corrie said.

At his mother's instruction, Marston obliged.

Knowing already that Marston was fourteen, Albert was surprised at how diminutive the boy was. But after running his gaze up and down the teenager, he realized he looked this way because of how he hunched over, as if carrying the weight of the world on his shoulders.

Feeling the awkwardness of the moment, Albert didn't

charge forward to embrace him. Instead, he extended his hand in a simple greeting, as he did for the courier who delivered his weekly stock.

Marston didn't take Albert's hand. The pale boy had yet to raise his eyes and acknowledge his presence, so maybe he hadn't noticed the proffered hand?

"He's a shy boy," Corrie said from alongside him. "He's happy to meet you though."

"Of course. We can't all be big talkers. I, myself, prefer a quiet room."

"He's not spoken much of late. Not since his father died."

"I'm sorry to hear that ... I really am." He stepped forward, and despite the inapproachable nature of the boy, he managed to force himself to place a hand on the rigid boy's shoulder. "I'm sorry for your loss, Marston."

The boy didn't pull away, which Albert was pleased about; however, he still hadn't looked up.

"It's hit him hard," Corrie said. "Are you not going to ask how it happened?"

Albert took his hand from Marston's shoulder. "It's none of my business, but if you want to talk about it, I'm listening."

"He died on the Great Day of Burning."

"Sorry?"

"The Great Day of Burning. It was the day when Griffin burned down the church that Pastor Alton Banks had erected in the Nucleus. We lost people in that church."

"I'm sorry. Was your husband in the fire?"

"No, your grandson's father, Sumner, died in what came next."

Albert gulped.

"Frank Yorke, do you know him?"

Albert turned away. "Yes ..."

"Did you help him?"

Albert stepped away from them both. He felt the threat of tears. "I didn't know."

"Didn't know his actions would cause an internal conflict that would split our land in two?"

Albert looked down.

"You must have known that what you did to Griffin's son would send the monster into a rage."

Albert looked up. "I didn't kill Griffin's son."

"But you burned his body to create the diversion that allowed Frank Yorke inside."

"Yes ..." Tears sprang to his eyes. "But ... I *didn't* know. I didn't know about you."

"You helped to fracture our land."

Albert turned and rubbed at his eyes. "If I'd known ... but your place, the Nucleus, it took from me ... it took from me the only thing I've ever loved." He looked between his grandson with his head hanging low and his daughter who looked like a commando with her shaven head. How badly damaged were these people, his closest living relatives? Because of him. Because of what he'd agreed to do with Frank.

She looked down at the steel track she stood on and rubbed at the corner of her eye with her palm. "I forgive you. You weren't to know ... Father."

He stepped forward, feeling hope blossoming inside himself. "Yes ... that's the truth. I didn't know. So, let me help you now ... Let me make up for it."

She kept her eyes down. "It's too late."

"Too late for what? Are you in danger?"

She nodded and glanced at her son.

Albert also looked across at Marston, who'd already

refocused on the iron door. "Leave the Nucleus now." Albert put a hand on her upper arm. "You and Marston come with me."

She shook her head and looked back up at him. "What will that solve?"

"I'll be able to keep you safe."

She shook her head.

"I've had to fend for myself a good while. I'm not a frail, old man."

"It's not that I'm worried about. It's my people I'm worried about. I can't leave them to what's coming."

"Coming? I don't understand—"

"Frank Yorke and Celestia are taking down our defenses."

"I don't understand."

He listened as she explained how they were disarming the Nucleus.

"We're all terrified," Celestia said. "*I'm* terrified. There are drones overhead—"

"*Shit* ... yes, I know." Albert sighed. "It's Sheriff Gordon Kane. He's planning to move on you. He asked me to help. You'll be please to know I sent him packing."

Corrie broke away from the hand on her arm and stepped backward, her hand over her mouth. "He asked *you* to help? How many people are helping him?"

"He only has three deputies. Apart from that, I don't know of any others. Hopefully, there aren't any. I don't think the four of them can take on the Nucleus alone!"

"Why did you refuse to help him? You didn't know about us."

Albert stepped forward. "Because of Frank. He's my friend. I'm not about to—"

"Frank is the problem! He's tearing down our walls so

they can finish us off."

"I can't believe that—"

"Believe it, *Father*. You can come and walk in through the southernmost forest right now if you don't. Nothing will stop you. All the traps are gone."

"Really? Why would he do that? He'd know that was a bad idea."

Corrie shrugged. "Come with me to the Nucleus, Father. Come and see."

"I ... I ..." Albert chewed his bottom lip. He tasted blood and stopped. "Is that really such a good idea?"

She turned toward the mine. "Marston, we have to go."

"Wait, wait!" Albert put up his palms. "Are you sure it's not best just to leave the Nucleus and come with me? Maybe what's going to happen is inevitable anyway? Even if Celestia and Frank are accelerating the outcome."

She glared at Albert. "Celestia plans to march into Brady Crossing and make peace during the next couple of days."

Albert's eyes widened. It sounded so ridiculous.

"I know, and *you* know, Father, that she's declaring open season on us."

Albert shook his head. He didn't want to believe this.

"Come on, Marston." Corrie stepped forward and put her arm around her boy's shoulders. She turned him. He looked so frail, like a decrepit old man with the face of a child.

They traversed the steel track, past the overturned cart.

Albert gulped. So, here it was, the mystery of his life finally revealed. He thought back to his store—a quiet life until the end of his days. He watched his departing family heading into fire and fury. "Wait! I'm coming."

At least fire and fury offered him a purpose.

8

Walker had warned that it would take an hour or so to wade through the trees and undergrowth that swamped the northernmost side of the hill. As they followed, Walker burbled to himself, rather manically. No doubt watching someone having their skull crushed as the starter to a main course, which was to have one's *own* skull crushed, had caused this.

Gordon and his three deputies, Brad, Scott and Riley, followed Walker in single file to ensure they didn't step on one of the yawning beartraps, of which they were many. All four had rifles slung over their shoulders.

Such was the state of Walker, Gordon kept expecting to hear the biting of metal on bone. As a result, he flinched every time a piece of bracken crunched under the fool's foot. It was intensely irritating.

"Forty minutes in, and I can see nothing but beartraps and deer shit," Gordon said.

His deputies laughed.

"It's not in anyone's interests to go faster," Walker said.

"My interests are the only interests that matter here,

84

Walker. But you can take your time. If you are tricking us, I want to kill you personally. I don't want you avalanching blood from standing on a trap and taking the easy way out."

Walker continued to lead them around the metal teeth. The traps were coming thicker and faster now.

"What do you hope to achieve when you get there?" Walker asked. "Rifle or no rifles, four of you won't be enough."

"You're right," Gordon said. "This is reconnaissance. The battle is for another day."

Walker grunted. "Even with strategy, you wouldn't stand a chance."

"Next time, we're coming back with an army. Anyway, keep an eye on where you're going. I need your legs intact for the walk home."

Walker mumbled something.

"What did you say, slug?" Gordon asked.

"I said, I'm glad I'm so important to you."

"You are, Walker. Don't underestimate how much."

* * *

Thaxton pressed the round pan in the middle of the beartrap with a stick, and the steel jaws broke it in two. "Eighteen." He scooped up the disarmed trap and placed it into a large rubble bag.

As each beartrap weighed over twenty pounds; he was only putting four into each rubble bag. He'd leave them dotted around so a group of them could lug them into the Focus later.

It felt strange doing this task alone. The other day, in the southernmost forest, there'd been five of them. But Everlyn and his colleagues had declined to come today. He knew why, of course. They'd decided that enough was enough, that further disarmament of the Nucleus was suicide.

He'd declined their invitation to stay back with them—not because he disagreed with them, but rather because Merithew had been his best friend, and Celestia had always been like family to him. He'd helped her out before, and he was more than willing to help her out again.

He picked up another branch and headed to his nineteenth beartrap of the day—

Snap!

Another beartrap had been activated in the distance.

He took a deep breath and reached down for his rifle beside the rubble bag.

"What the fuck?" Gordon hissed, surveying the closed beartrap, and turned around.

Directly behind him, Riley's red face spoke volumes.

"What did you?"

"Sorry, boss. I was checking my cell, and I ... I dropped it." He gestured into the closed beartrap. "Do you think it's bust?"

Imbecile. "What the fuck do you think?" Gordon shook his head. "Why've you got your goddamned cell out, Riley?"

"I needed to let my ma know what time I'll be back for dinner."

Scott and Brad sniggered.

"Well, I hope you got your message off," Gordon said, "before you potentially blew our mission."

Riley gulped and shook his head, slowly. "Actually, there was no reception."

The other deputies laughed again.

Gordon turned back, muttering, "Give me strength."

Walker snorted. "I can see why you need an army."

Gordon touched the back of his head with the muzzle of his rifle. "Get a fucking move on—" Up ahead, Gordon saw movement. *"Shit!"*

Gunfire erupted.

Thunk! A shower of splinters from a nearby trunk peppered Gordon's face.

*"*Take cover!" Gordon called.

His three deputies didn't need a second warning. Throwing caution to the wind regarding the traps, they dove behind trees.

Walker, sensing his opportunity, threw himself forward into a sprint.

Gordon went to his knees as the tall man poked around the tree to fire again.

Thud!

More splinters sprayed Gordon.

Gordon raised his rifle and kept it trained on the exact spot where the man's head and torso had appeared only moments ago. From the corner of his eye, he saw Walker fleeing but resisted the urge to turn the rifle on that bastard's back; first, he had to rid himself of the immediate danger. He pinned his eye to the crosshair. *Come on, you sono-fabitch ...* A clear understanding that his assailant could emerge from the *other* side of the tree gripped his heart coldly. *Don't waver ... trust your instincts. Come on, you sonofa—*

The man chose the same spot again, and the force of Gordon's bullet flung him backward.

"Walker!" Gordon shouted at the fleeing figure. "Stop or I'll shoot you in the goddamned back!"

His warning only seemed to spurn Walker on, who was weaving around traps as he retreated.

Fuck! Fuck! "Riley, this is your fault." Gordon looked back. "Get the hell after him!"

Riley emerged from behind the tree. His pale face and lack of urgency a clear indicator that this was one order he didn't want to follow.

"Now!"

"Yes, Sheriff," Riley said, looking as if he would vomit. He sprinted past his kneeling boss.

"Someone go with him. I'd go myself, but these legs aren't what they once were."

And they actually weren't. Even now, he was struggling to stand.

"I'll go!" Brad shouted and took off after Riley, who would seriously need to quicken his pace if he were to have any hope of catching Walker.

"Sheriff," Scott said, coming alongside him, and offering his hand.

Gordon took it. He grunted as he stood. "We fucked this up."

"Hopefully, we can put it right."

"Well, we can't make it any worse—"

They heard the snap of a trap, and Brad tumbled, screaming.

* * *

Albert's eyes widened when the sentry, Lyman, activated the rising arm barrier for Corrie's pickup at the entrance. "I thought no one got in the Nucleus—no one alive, that is."

"Things have changed." Corrie glanced at her son in the back seat, who'd been staring out the window the whole journey, grey as a ghost. "Besides, Lyman understands what's happening here. He's on our side."

"What does he understand?"

"That our world is in grave danger." She drove through the barrier onto a dirt path.

"Where do I come in?"

"With the knowledge of what the sheriff is planning in Mossbark. You simply must tell them what you've told me. You are the evidence that Celestia's way is not the way. The rest, I believe, will be easy."

"I do not want to be involved in any violence, Corrie ..."

"Then, why the rifle?"

"I've just crossed the border of the Nucleus. I'm just keeping up appearances that I'm not completely suicidal."

After parking, Corrie and Marston led Albert toward a small community of wooden cabins and children playing in carefully tended gardens.

His eyes widened yet again.

"This is the Focus," Corrie said.

As they marched through this area, reaction from the residents was mixed. Some who were dressed in their usual loose-fitting drab cotton clothing merely continued gardening, playing with their children, or skinning freshly caught deer, while offering a brief nod and a suspicious look. While others walked straight up to Corrie and demanded to know who he was.

"My father. My mother found love in the cesspit that is Brady Crossing—of all places."

One man, who wore an apron splattered with the blood of a deer, pointed at her. Albert noticed, with disgust, some of the fur glued to the blood on his hand. "So, you're a half-breed, Corrie?" the butcher asked.

"I am, Leander. Does that cause you concern?"

"Depends."

"Depends on what?"

"On this outsider you've just escorted in."

Albert tightened his hand on the rifle strap across his chest, suddenly glad he had brought it.

"He brings information to share with our people," Corrie said.

"I see. Go on, then. Share."

"Come to the square in thirty minutes. Bring as many people as you can round up."

Leander narrowed his eyes and regarded her for a moment, before giving her a cautious nod. He then turned.

Albert looked at Corrie. "I don't seem to have made a good impression—"

A gunshot.

"Hunting?" Albert said.

"Not at this time. It is forbidden this early. This way ..." Corrie pointed toward the woods and ran.

After hearing the gunshot, Celestia spun from the burned-out church and jabbed her finger off into the distance. "The forest ... *Thaxton!*" she yelled and ran.

Jake shouted after her, "We're unarmed! Let the soldiers handle it ..."

Celestia ignored him and picked up speed.

Jake watched the scheming soldiers dart from the square. They were nearer to the northernmost forest than Celestia and would surely get there first. He felt some relief, but not enough to stop him giving chase. A strong runner, and much taller than Celestia, he closed the gap to her, and they drew side by side in the square.

* * *

Albert reached the forest's edge.

Corrie's hand shot out to stop him. "The traps haven't all been disarmed here."

Albert leaned over, clutching his knees, gulping air.

"Give me your rifle," Corrie said.

Albert shook his head, straightening himself. He sucked in some more air and managed to speak. "I've only just found you ..." Another breath. "I'm not going to risk you." He glanced behind him and saw his grandson Marston hadn't followed. That was something, at least.

He turned back in time to see a man burst from behind a tree, ten yards or so ahead. Albert raised his rifle.

The man was coming at some speed. If Corrie's warning regarding the traps were true, the man was skating on thin ice.

The shopkeeper put the sight to his eye.

"No!" Corrie yanked down his rifle. "It's Walker! He's one of us. *Walker!*"

"Yes!" the running man shouted. "I'm not alone; they're be—"

Another gunshot. It was as if Walker was shoved in the back. With his chest thrust out and his arms flailing, he went to the ground.

Corrie started forward.

"Corrie!" Albert shouted.

She continued, clearly determined to reach the injured man writhing on the ground.

With the sight pinned to his eye, Albert swept the rifle in an arc over the trees ahead, seeking out the gunman. "Corrie, get back here!"

She closed the gap between her and Walker. She fell to her knees beside him and took hold of his head.

Then Albert saw the gunman burst from the undergrowth with a rifle raised.

As a child, Albert had often hunted with his father and had been a great shot. He fired, hoping old age hadn't dampened his aim. His shot was as true as ever.

The man's head snapped backward, and he fell back into the undergrowth.

The old man kept the gun on the woods in case anybody else made an appearance.

"Walker's dead," Corrie called back.

"Okay," Albert said, hearing people running up behind him. "Now, get back here, please." He felt the muzzle of a gun pressing against the back of his head.

"Who are you?" a woman asked.

It took some effort for Gordon and Scott to pry open the jaws. Brad moaned the whole time. For good reason. His foot was hanging loose.

Scott tasted bile when he examined the remains of his brother's mangled ankle and the blood spewing from it. "Hold on, Brad. Do you hear? You hold the *fuck* on." He tore off his beige deputy shirt, revealing a short-sleeved vest. "This is going to hurt like hell, little brother, but I have to stop the bleeding."

"Don't call me that!" Brad hissed between clenched teeth. "We're twins, for fuck's sake!"

"You were born second, brother." He tied the shirt just above Brad's ruined ankle. He tightened his makeshift tourniquet as best he could, while Brad groaned. "And don't you forget that."

"Shush, both of you," Gordon said. "I need to listen."

Scott noticed Gordon staring into the distance, listening to the distant sound of a growing crowd.

"We have to go, now," Gordon said.

"What about Riley?" Scott asked.

"He's done. Did you hear those shots? We go *now*."

Scott moved over so he was alongside Brad. "Arm around me, Brad—"

"No," Gordon said. "Leave him."

"What?" Scott felt his brother's arm loop around his neck.

"He'll slow us down. They'll catch us. Then we all die."

"I'm taking that chance."

Gordon raised his rifle and pointed it at Brad's head. "Give me the nod. Far better he goes now, quickly, than at the hands of these savages."

Scott scrunched his face at Gordon. He no longer recognized this man. "Boss, I got this."

"You're a fool."

"You go on ahead. This is my risk."

"Suit yourself. Don't say I didn't warn you," Gordon said and started off into the forest.

"Hold on, Brad. Hold onto me with everything you got." Scott started to rise. "Don't make a sound ..."

Scott felt his brother's body trembling under the force of trying to lock away a guttural cry. Some of it broke free, but this was understandable. The agony must have been indescribable.

93

Scott locked his arm around his brother's waist for extra support. "Are you ready?"

"I don't—"

"You got this, little brother."

"Don't fucking call—"

"Come on!" Scott started to hoist his brother forward.

"This is going to be too slow."

"We must go slow. There're traps everywhere, and we haven't got Walker anymore."

Scott recalled the patterns of the traps. It was safer to leave as much space as possible between them and the trees, as most of the traps congregated around the trunks, so he dragged his brother onward, keeping his gaze firmly on the ground to look for those glints of metal and ensure they always kept several feet from every approaching tree.

9

Everlyn, Fern, and Glynnie stood beside the bodies of their two dead soldiers. They'd carried Thaxton and Walker from the edge of the northernmost forest and into the square. There they had placed the fallen heroes, in the center, for the community to gather around and acknowledge the evil that had been visited on their land.

At first, agitated chatter rose among the gathering crowd, which included the children. However, the arrival and anguished scream of Thaxton's wife, Cathanne, reduced everyone to silence.

She barged through the crowd and looked down at her husband. "Thaxton!" She fell to her knees and took his lifeless hand, before pressing her own face to his cold cheek.

Corrie supressed a smile. This was going much better than she'd hoped. She touched Albert's arm to get his attention.

He nodded, indicating he was ready, but didn't look at her, and his grey face suggested he was far from steady.

She wasn't surprised. After being forced to shoot the

intruder, Everlyn had held a gun to his head. If Corrie hadn't sprinted back from the Walker's corpse in that instant, she'd may well have been too late in steadying Everlyn's hand.

Corrie led Albert to the raised platform at the edge of the square, where Celestia had stood several days prior, admitting to the killing of the elders and providing just cause. Corrie ascended the steps to the platform, Albert just behind her.

Meanwhile, Cathanne tilted her head back, looked up, and screamed, "Who killed Thaxton?"

The crowd edged backward.

"Celestia!" Corrie called out.

The crowd turned as one to face the platform.

"She killed him the moment she lowered our defenses."

"You're not safe here, anymore," Celestia said to Jake at the table in her cabin.

"Neither of us are."

Jake recalled the chaos at the edge of the northernmost forest: the soldiers arguing among themselves over their best course of action while others dragged the bodies from the undergrowth. But what had been most startling for Jake had been the presence of Albert and the revelation he had shared with him:

"Albert?"

The old man had turned to look at him, but there was no warm look; instead, it was a similar look to the one he'd received on first arriving in Mossbark all those months ago and striding into Hardy Conveniences—cold and full of contempt.

"Why are you here?" Jake asked him.

"You've made a mistake, Frank. A *huge* mistake. You don't understand what you're doing here."

Jake creased his brow. "Explain, Albert. Please."

"What happened here is only just the beginning. There're more coming. Many more."

"When did you ever care about this place? And again, what the hell are you doing here? I'm struggling to make any sense."

"Why?" Corrie stepped forward and put a hand on Albert's shoulder. "My father is making complete sense."

Father ... Jake's eyes widened.

"He's here to help tidy up the mess that you and this child have caused."

Celestia bit. "Watch how you talk about your leader, Corrie."

"Father?" Jake asked Albert, still stuck on his friend's revelation. "How can that be—"

"You're *not* my leader, Celestia," Corrie said and nodded at Everlyn.

Everlyn and Ibre closed in on either side of Celestia and Jake with their rifles raised.

"So, this is how you choose to express your discontent?" Celestia asked Everlyn. "By becoming a traitor."

"You were warned," Everlyn said. "Look what has happened."

"Take them back to their cabin," Corrie said. "And Ibre?"

"Yes?"

"Stand guard."

"What the hell are you doing, Corrie?" Celestia asked.

"I'm going to lead a meeting in the square ... so we can decide what to do with you."

* * *

They'd been sitting at the table for almost twenty minutes.

"Fuck this," Jake said, standing. "I'm not dying on my arse."

"Sit tight. My people will see sense."

Will they? Jake thought, imagining the events in the woods would have been enough to send most of the thirty or so remaining residents spiraling into the depths of paranoia. He approached the front door of the cabin.

"Don't be stupid, Jake. Ibre will shoot you."

"We're out of options." He lifted his hand to knock.

"No, wait ..." Celestia said. "There's another way."

Jake looked back at her.

She was shaking her head. "I still think it's best to—"

"The other way?"

"Behind the television, in my room. The slats are loose. It's where I used to sneak in to avoid my father when I'd broken curfew."

"Wait here."

She stood. "No. If you're going to create a shit storm, I want to be in the center of it with you."

* * *

"What do we stand for?" Corrie asked from the platform, scanning the crowd.

Heads fell.

"What do we stand for when we allow *this* to happen to the people who we love?"

She waited.

"Does no one want to answer?"

Leander, the man who had challenged Corrie earlier for bringing Albert into the Nucleus, stepped forward. "Where's Celestia? Where's our leader?"

"She's in her cabin. She'll remain there until we decide how to proceed."

"Until we decide," Leander said, "or you?"

Corrie shook her head. "You misunderstand the situation, Leander. I'm not standing here with any intention of a power grab. I'm simply identifying a problem—a problem that we, *yourself* included, Leander, are all aware of, a problem that threatens our existence." She looked across the crowd again. "Yet, if all of you here stand with Leander, in his call to bring back Celestia, then I will not stop that. However, I fear you'll be ignoring the events of today for what they are: a great warning of the horrors to come." She put her hand on Albert's shoulder. "My mother strayed from the Nucleus, and this man, Albert, is my father by blood." She allowed a nervous chatter to spread through the crowd before interrupting them. "He stands here with my best interests at heart. And therefore, yours. Listen to what he has to say."

After escaping via the loose slats in Celestia's room and evading Ibra who'd been standing at the cabin door, Jake and Celestia headed toward the square and entered the Pinnacle through its back door. The Pinnacle was a large structure which catered for events, parties, and served as a meeting place when the rains were heavy.

Carefully, in case anyone was occupying the place, Jake and Celestia weaved to the front of the cabin, avoiding seating areas, a makeshift bar, and a dancefloor. When they reached the front windows that looked over the square, they crouched beneath them and peered above the sill. They wouldn't be seen. The crowd were a fair distance away, fixated on the raised platform, on which Corrie was standing next to a man addressing the audience.

Jake shook his head, for the world was a strange place. Albert, father to a resident of a place he despised, was warning the Nucleus of a great threat to their existence.

"Gordon will not stop until the Nucleus is gone." Albert stood back, indicating he'd concluded.

"I can't believe it," Jake whispered to Celestia. "Is it even true? Is Corrie really Albert's *child*?"

"I don't know," Celestia said. "I really don't."

Corrie stepped forward. "You have been sold a lie." She pointed at an elderly man at the front of the crowd. "Do you see that now, Leander?"

Leander nodded and, head lowered, turned and sauntered back to the rest of the audience. As he did so, the soldiers, led by Everlyn, marched toward the platform.

"Merithew tore everything down! Griffin trampled it underfoot! And now, Celestia is sweeping the pieces of our once-great land into the fire! I propose we return to how it was before, to what Althea promised us."

Jake felt Celestia grip his arm.

"How do we all feel about this?" Corrie asked the crowd.

Jake scanned the multitude of faces as they flicked back

and forth, regarding one another. He didn't need to wait for the response. He knew what was coming.

Celestia's grip tightened.

Boots thumped on steps as Everlyn ascended them to the platform, Fern and Glynnie following closely behind. Ibre would still be standing outside Celestia's cabin, none the wiser to their escape.

"How do we feel?" Corrie raised her voice.

"Let's go back to how it was!" someone shouted.

"Is it only you, *Olin*?" Corrie asked, nodding. "Or does anyone else want to speak up?"

Celestia's grip was hurting Jake's arm now.

"I agree!" someone called.

"Thank you, *Nella*. Only two of you, though? Look down at your dead brothers. Thaxton and Walker. Look down at them, people of the Nucleus, and tell me how it should be!"

Jake put his hand on Celestia's.

"Me too!"

"Yes, me!"

"And me!"

"We have to leave," Jake said, looking at Celestia to his right side. He waited for her response, but she simply stared through the window.

Jake turned back as Everlyn and the two soldiers fanned out on the platform behind Corrie and Albert, while, one by one, the people in the crowd hollered out their support.

A cry came from the man she'd called Leander. "Back to the old ways!"

Another shout came from the woman she'd called Nella. "Death to outsiders!"

Corrie nodded and repeated, "Death to outsiders."

The crowd sprung to life and chanted, *"Death to outsiders!"*

"Being one of said outsiders, I'm quite eager to leave now." Jake eyed Celestia again.

The young girl, who'd only ever wanted the best for her people, had tears streaming down her face.

* * *

"Death to outsiders!"

Albert gulped and looked at his daughter beside him.

She met his eyes, smiled, and mouthed, *Thank you.*

"Death to outsiders!"

Was he one of the outsiders? "Am I—"

She pressed a finger to her mouth, and he stopped. She grabbed his upper arm with her left hand. She maintained eye contact with him and gave him a swift nod.

He took it as reassurance. *God, how you look like your mother.*

"Death to outsiders!"

Keeping her left hand on his upper arm, she raised her right hand in the air. The crowd settled quickly, until silence settled like a blanket over the square.

"I want to thank Albert Hardy, *my father*, for bringing us the truth." She spoke loudly to the crowd as she kept her gaze on Albert. "Without his words, we may not stand as ready as we currently do."

Albert broke his daughter's eye contact to look across the crowd all staring up at him with stern faces. A knot tightened in his stomach.

"Without him, I may even have fallen back in the woods."

Every pair of eyes in the crowd bored into him.

Albert tasted bile in the back of his throat.

Corrie retracted her hand from his arm. "But he's an outsider. And I will prove my commitment to the old ways now." She turned her head to the three soldiers fanned out behind them and gave a swift nod.

They closed in quickly, and before he could risk his neck by jumping from the platform, two of the bastards had locked onto his arms. "Stop—"

The crowd drowned out his protests with a cheer.

He tried to pull himself loose, but he was no match for his younger and stronger assailants.

They turned him to face the baying crowd.

Corrie stepped in front of him. "An outsider here is evidence of the frailty brought by Celestia."

"You brought me in!" Albert shouted.

He wasn't heard over the crowd, who was chanting, *"Outsider! Outsider! Outsider!"*

Corrie turned to face him so her back was to the crowd.

He shook his head. "How could you?"

The third soldier stepped forward and placed a knife into Corrie's hands.

Albert's blood ran cold; it was a gutting knife.

"Outsider! Outsider! Outsider!"

"What about Marston?" Albert asked, shaking. "He's watching! My grandson is watching."

She was close enough to hear him over the chant of the crowd, but she didn't respond.

"I'm your father, Corrie!"

"Outsider! Outsider! Outsider!"

She leaned in and hissed, "And I thank you, Father, for endearing me to them." She tore apart his cotton shirt. The buttons gave easily.

He fought against the soldier's grip, but it was useless,

and he eventually slumped in their hold, out of breath. Tears welled in the corners of his eyes as he looked into the eyes of the daughter he didn't know existed until yesterday. *Those eyes. Blue and green. They're mine. And those dimples in the cheeks. They're Roseleigh's. Such beautiful dimples—*

He felt pressure on his belly. He let his head fall back as the searing pain kicked in. The shout of the crowds and his own screams thankfully drowned out the sounds of the blade chewing its way through his stomach.

When his daughter stepped away from him, the soldiers released him, and he stumbled forward, clutching his guts, staring at the crowd as his vision blurred. He thought he could still hear their chanting, but he couldn't be certain, because everything was fading fast. He saw her again— beautiful, soft-skinned Roseleigh smiling across a crowded room of drunken, tired miners at young Albert Hardy. Local rebel. The boy who'd told his father to stick the convenience store—the family business—where the sun doesn't shine. He was going down into the pits with the boys he'd grown up with.

"Roseleigh." He stumbled to the edge of the platform. "Roseleigh, why did you choose me?"

He fell.

* * *

Albert's entrails spilled from his body when he hit the floor.

Jake turned, clutching his mouth. He retched a couple of times and scurried backward from the window. "Jesus ... Jesus ..." He looked at Celestia, who now had her forehead against the window.

He retched again, but then he shook his head. *Get yourself together, Jake.* It wasn't the time to wallow in revulsion and despair. He rose to a crouch, moved back toward her, and eased her from the window. Her eyes were closed. He put his arm around her shoulder. "We go now."

"I ... I—"

"Listen, Celestia. Listen to me right now. We go this second, or we'll be next."

She opened her eyes, sucked in a deep breath, and turned to look at him. "The southernmost forest."

*"*Good call."

And it was. Not only because they didn't need to cross the square to get to the Focus, but because that side had already been disarmed. They left the baying crowd as it fell under the spell of a new leader.

10

While Brad bled out on the back seat, Scott rode shotgun, watching his boss's expression twisting and turning as God knows what went through his messed-up mind.

His brother had been accurate in yesterday's assessment. Sheriff Gordon Kane had lost control.

"My hip flask, son ..." Gordon lifted a hand from the steering wheel to point at the glovebox.

"Sheriff, Riley is dead, my brother's a mess—"

"My *hip flask*, son." Gordon took his eyes from the road and froze Scott with them instead.

Scott popped the glovebox.

Brad moaned from the back.

After Scott had handed Gordon the silver container, he turned and reached for his pale brother's arm. He squeezed it gently. "Not long, Brad. Hold on. They'll get you as good as new."

Or they'll have that foot off as soon as they see it.

Scott watched Gordon swill from his flask before offering it over. "Have some, son. You need it."

Scott shook his head. "I need to stay steady for Brad."

Gordon tapped his steering wheel. "Riley was a goddamned fool for dropping his cell, but, you know, we can *still* do this." He smiled. "I mean, we got out just fine, didn't we? We didn't need a guide."

"Please!" Brad wailed from the back. "I can't take it anymore!"

Gordon continued, "Don't draw too close to the tree trunks and avoid patches of undergrowth. All the traps that don't follow the pattern are clear to see anyway."

"You can't be serious about going back there," Scott said, wincing as his brother gave another guttural moan from the back seat. "I mean, *ever*?"

Gordon smiled at him again. "Sooner rather than later, son. We have them on the ropes."

"We don't know that!"

"Did they chase us? They're on their last *fucking* legs!"

They approached a rotary. Scott sighed when he saw the signpost pointing left for the hospital. "Almost there, little brother."

"Fuck you with the little—" Brad hissed.

Gordon drove straight over the rotary.

"What are you doing?" Scott asked, raising his voice.

"I'm making a sensible decision."

"Have you seen Brad?"

"Son, I need you to calm down. This was why I suggested a drink. We take Brad to the hospital with his foot hanging off, what do you think'll happen?"

"They'll stop the bleeding!"

Gordon hit a pothole. The vehicle jolted, and Brad wailed from the back seat.

"Bad idea," Gordon said. "We'll have MSP up our asses before sundown."

"Would that be such a bad thing?" Scott said. "We're struggling! We need help to finish the Nucleus."

"I think you're forgetting what is back at the station, son."

He was, of course, referring to Leo—or, at least, *what* was left of Leo.

Scott threw the hipflask into the glovebox and slammed it shut. He stared ahead but could see Gordon shaking his head from the corner of his eye. His brother continued to moan, incessantly.

"You want the state troopers marching in while you're scrubbing the cell floor?" Gordon asked.

Scott clenched his fists on his lap. "I'm not letting my brother die."

"You need to *calm* down, son. No one is dying around here. Riley is the last man we lose. I know a doctor in Lewis. I will bring him to the station; he can treat Brad."

"Treat him? His foot is hanging off! He needs a hospital!"

Another pothole, another scream.

"I've made up my mind, son. And when you calm down, you'll realize this is for the best. After we've disposed of Leo, helped your brother, we need to be ready to go back into that vile place. We finish this *ourselves*."

"Just the two of us?" Scott guffawed.

"No, son. What do you think I've been doing these last weeks? I've been speaking to the people of Mossbark! Not surprisingly, the majority want rid of the rotten core now that the money has dried up. That's good hunting land up there. And without that scourge, we can work on tourism too. Albert and a few others refused flat out, of course, but tradesmen like Nicholas Brannagh and John Reeves are ready. I easily have ten men who I can take in with us. And now that we know how, what's stopping us?"

"And do what? Kill them?" Scott said, shaking. Unable to resist the hipflask any longer, he took a gulp and winced. "Madness."

"We drive them off our land," Gordon said. "They can go where the hell they please, but they're leaving Mossbark."

"And when they refuse to leave?"

Gordon snorted. "Why? It'd be suicide! They're weak, vulnerable. This is the best chance we'll ever have."

"Scott," Brad called from the back. "I'm so fucking cold back here."

Scott took another mouthful and winced. "Not long now, brother."

Gordon put a hand on Scott's knee. "Trust me, son. I'll get Brad help. Do we have a deal?"

"And if I say no, boss?"

"You won't, son. Because if all three of us go to that hospital, we'll be in the system by sunrise." Gordon shook his head. "And then what'll have been the point of all of this?"

Even though they had already disarmed the southernmost forest, Jake stayed away from the trees and out of the undergrowth as they fled the Nucleus in case the now-deceased Thaxton had missed one. He also made Celestia run behind him so she wasn't at any risk.

Breathless most of the journey, they didn't speak much. A good thing. The execution of Albert had been one of the most atrocious things either of them had ever witnessed. To reflect on it, to *dwell* on it, wouldn't help with an escape.

After they burst from the edge of the forest, Celestia fell to her knees by the road that led into Brady Crossing and vomited.

Jake knelt beside her and placed a hand on her shoulder.

She turned to smile at him, a string of saliva dangling from her bottom lip. "Sorry."

"For what?"

She nodded down at the pool of vomit. "I thought I was stronger than this."

"You're strong."

She shook her head. "Look what I caused."

Jake squeezed her shoulder. "You aren't responsible for psychotic behavior like that."

Celestia pulled away from him. "No, admit it, Jake. You thought I was wrong. All along, you said it."

"Even if I did disagree at the time, what difference does it make? Decisions must be made. It is normal for views to differ. But you were the leader of this place, and I supported you. I *still* support you."

"She just ... *you saw!*"

"And you think that is down to your decision to form a relationship with the towns that surround you? Do you really believe this wouldn't have happened anyway?"

"Mossbark will seize this opportunity now. They'll come and finish us off. I blew it."

"They were coming anyway. I respect you for at least trying. I respect you for being true to yourself, to try to bring peace."

"I was too impetuous! Taking down the traps—what the hell was I thinking?"

"They didn't even come through this side! As I said, Celestia, you have done nothing but try to save a community that can't be saved. I'm afraid, ultimately, that is the truth." He helped her to her feet.

"So, now what?"

"We are alone. It is time for you to accept that. But don't worry, I am reasonably experienced at this."

They walked adjacent to the road in the shadows of the trees.

"Surely Brady Crossing is not a good idea?"

"I have to pick up my money so we can get out of here. It's hidden in the motel room I was staying in."

"Won't we be seen?"

"Well, you won't be, because you're not coming to the motel room."

"So, where do I go?"

"I have somewhere safe in mind. You'll be able to get some rest."

As they neared town, Jake tried to turn on his cellphone. Obviously, it didn't work. It had been turned off for too long and was out of charge.

* * *

After admonishing Ibre for letting Celestia and the outsider slip through his fingers, Everlyn entered Celestia's cabin.

Corrie was sitting at the table, scrubbing her fingernails with a damp towel. She didn't look up.

Everlyn firmly closed the door behind her.

It didn't work; Corrie still didn't look up.

"Corrie?" Everlyn asked.

"My father's blood." Corrie scrubbed hard at her nail with an old towel.

"We need to talk."

Corrie smiled. "Can you believe that old bastard, Merithew, used to live here? Eat his meals at this table?"

Everlyn stepped forward so the edge of table pressed against her thighs. "We need a plan."

"A disgrace, wasn't he?" Corrie scrubbed. "Merithew?"

"Actually, no. At the beginning, he was a good leader."

"At the beginning?" Corrie chortled. "You have a better memory than me." She threw down the towel. "Fuck it. What's a little bit of blood?" She finally looked up at Everlyn. "My father?"

"Being buried as you requested."

"Good. He deserves respect."

"Yes, after all, he certainly succeeded."

"Succeeded in what?"

"Bringing you power."

Corrie chortled again. "That was never his intention."

"But it was yours, wasn't it?"

"I see." Corrie smiled. "Is that why you've come to me now so quickly, Everlyn, to test my new power?"

"Why would I do that? If anything, I'm here to thank you. Because of you, the greatest threat we have ever faced to our survival is gone."

Corrie narrowed her eyes. "Gone ... but not dead."

"Gone is enough. She won't return."

"Still. Closure is good." Corrie rose from her seat. She stepped around the table and up close to Everlyn.

Everlyn didn't like having her personal space invaded, but nor was she about to challenge the Nucleus's new hero. And they had roared for her outside. Really *roared*.

Corrie was the same height as Everlyn, so the tip of her nose was close to hers. "Why do you come to me with your rifle?"

Everlyn touched the strap across her chest. "No reason. I'm never without it."

"A good leader doesn't need to carry a weapon. A good leader relies on their words."

"Then, I'm no leader if leaving myself vulnerable is a necessary qualification."

"I disagree, Everlyn. You lead those soldiers well. Your weapon is merely an accessory. You have nothing to fear from any of our men and women." Corrie pressed a hand to Everlyn's cheek.

Everlyn could smell the blood of Corrie's dead father.

"Do you have aspirations to be more than you are?"

"If you mean, do I want to lead the Nucleus? Then, no. The people do not want me. They want *you*."

"Do *you* want me?" Corrie leaned even closer so the tips of their noses were only several inches apart.

Everlyn swallowed.

"Do you?" Corrie asked.

"Yes."

"Good." Corrie dropped her hand from Everlyn's face and turned. She returned to the table and sat. "So, do you want to hear my ideas on how we can get ourselves out of the bother that Celestia has got us into?"

"I do, Corrie."

"Well, ready your soldiers, leader. It's time we took matters into our own hands rather than sitting here like fucking ducks."

11

Scott emptied the bloody water into the sink, refilled the mop bucket with fresh water and bleach, and raced down the line of cells, mopping his brow with the back of his wrist. He glanced into a cell at his moaning brother, Brad, as he writhed on the bed where Leo had choked on his own vomit. "Hold on, little brother."

Brad didn't respond to his playful banter. He was too far gone and in dire need of the doctor that the sheriff had promised. Gordon had been crystal clear though. Any evidence of the bloodbath involving Leo needed to be wiped away before they could welcome anybody into the station.

"You think your brother will thank you if he has to recover in a prison hospital?" Gordon had asked just before leaving. *"You know what happens to cops in prison?"*

You could have at least helped clean, Gordon. After all, it was you who crushed Leo's skull and made the fucking mess!

Scott stepped over Leo's corpse, which he'd already tightly taped up with trash bags. He rolled the bucket to the side and knelt beside the entrance to the cell in the spot where Leo had died. Scott had been mopping frantically for a while now, and the damp floor glistened, but the red tinge was starting to disappear.

"Daddy ..." Brad said. "You told me to pick it up ... I didn't know it would spill everywhere ..."

"Snap out of it, Brad. You're seeing things," Scott said, pulling a towel from his shoulder. With his gloved hands, he worked the towel into the runner, scooping out small fragments of bone and grey matter. "This is fucking disgusting." Once he'd gathered all the debris, he threw it and the towel into another trash bag. He stood and went to work on the floor and the runner with the mop again.

"Please let me out, Daddy ... It's so dark ... I can't see my hands."

"Jeez, shut up Brad," Scott said, cleaning furiously, dripping with sweat. "I'm trying my best here."

Scott worked until the cell no longer looked like a crime scene to the naked eye. Obviously, if someone went to work with Luminol on this cell floor, they would have a field day, but he doubted that was likely to happen any time soon, and he planned to scrub it daily with bleach until it was no longer a problem.

Meanwhile, Brad plead with their dead father, pausing occasionally to scream out in pain.

Scott took a deep breath, knelt, and got his hands around the wrapped corpse.

This was going to be a nightmare.

Grunting, he dragged the body to the back door of the station where his pickup waited.

* * *

After weighting down Leo's body with rocks, Scott sank him in the River Beech. He'd picked a spot on the river some distance from Brady Crossing, away from wandering eyes. He returned to his pickup and changed from his sweat- and blood-stained uniform into the spare he always carried with him in his trunk. He shoved the incriminating clothes into another trash bag and cast his gaze across the river. Sinking these garments here by the body would be mindless stupidity. He determined to burn them later in his back yard.

It took ten minutes for Scott to reach civilization again and pick up enough bars on his cell to contact the retired doctor Gordon had given him the number for.

The doctor sounded old, and Scott was worried he'd have to beg him to come and save his brother's life.

It wasn't necessary. He was a good friend to Gordon and owed him a debt for a service that had saved his career many years ago.

Scott wasn't in the least bit curious as to what that was; recent events had desensitized him. He knew his boss was capable of anything.

The doctor said he would be with him in less than thirty minutes.

When Scott entered the station via the same door he'd left through, he knew immediately that his brother was dead. It wasn't the silence, or even the cold feeling of emptiness in the station that told him this. He just *simply* knew. Losing a twin was not like losing a brother, someone had once told him. It seemed they'd been right after all.

His instinct was to run, but he knew it was too late.

Plus, the acrid smell of bleach reminded him that the floor could still be damp and hazardous.

Despite knowing it was futile, he couldn't help himself. "Brad. I'm back." He reached the cell where Walker had been in. "The doctor is on his way."

With a cold sensation spreading through his stomach, he turned into his brother's cell and saw that his instinct had been right. He approached, fell to his knees, and placed a hand on his brother's. *Still warm. Have I only just missed your final breath?*

Brad's eyes were open and unmoving. His mouth had stretched back over his teeth.

"Little brother, I'm sorry."

When it became clear to Scott that Brad would never admonish him for calling him little brother again, his world really did start to rock. He moved from his knees in a sitting position, still clutching his brother's stiffening hand, and tried to slow down his breathing. After he regained control, he slipped his cellphone from his pocket, and canceled the old doctor's visit.

The old doctor was, of course, mystified, but Scott had no appetite to offer him any satisfaction, so he ended the call quickly.

He kissed his cold brother's forehead. "Goodbye, little brother." He rose to his feet. "Fuck you, Gordon," he said and headed off to contact the Maine State Police.

* * *

"What a cluster fuck," Susan said.

Gordon closed the office door to try to shut out his dead wife's voice, despite knowing she resided in his head.

"A reconnaissance mission?" she continued. "And the

result? A dead officer, another with his foot hanging off, and your magic ticket into the Nucleus? Walker? A bullet in his back!"

"We got out without Walker; we can get in too ... There's a method to the traps." He pressed his back against the closed office door to stop Susan making an entrance, despite knowing she was a rotting corpse in the other room.

He drank another glass of whiskey. This was the most effective way of shutting her out. He winced and let the alcohol do its work. He stepped away from the door, and when he couldn't hear her anymore, he pulled his cellphone from his pocket and stared at it.

He scrolled through to Nicholas Brannagh. As he thought of the burly man carving up carcasses in Mossbark butcher's shop, he held his finger above the call button. Then he shook his head. Nicholas was a stubborn old bastard, and without a guide, he wouldn't risk tapdancing around beartraps.

So he scrolled through to John Reeves, who had opened a new vape shop three doors down from Brannagh. Reeves was a loose cannon who'd earned the nickname Raging Reeves due to his temper and had a glass eye following a poor show in a bar brawl several years back. Gordon suspected that Raging Reeves would be more willing to 'go over the top' despite the risks.

Still, they would need more than just a borderline psychopath. He slipped his cellphone into his pocket. No, unless he found some reassurance that the way into the Rotten Core wasn't problematic, then the willing volunteers he'd amassed so far may frustrate him by biding their time.

He thought of Leo, Riley, Brad, and Susan.

No. Time was something he didn't have much of.

He turned his attention to his personal computer which

hummed in the corner of the room and wondered. Only yesterday, he'd sent Brad to fly the drone over the Nucleus. Brad had emailed the video file to Gordon, but he'd been too preoccupied to watch them. Scrutinizing the footage now may give him a moment of inspiration.

He paused to listen out for the criticism from Susan, designed to shatter his confidence. When it didn't come, he smiled. He took another swig of whiskey to keep her at bay, logged on to his computer, and launched his email to open the video footage that Brad had forwarded.

He sat back and watched as the drone swooped over the northernmost forest where he'd been involved in a bloody confrontation earlier. The camera panned over the square, then the residential area, before moving over the southernmost forest, and his heart skipped a beat. He paused the footage and slowly rewound to the moment the drone had hovered over a break in the canopy. He magnified the image to reveal a large man poking a stick into a beartrap, causing it to snap shut.

He continued the footage until he spotted something else in another part of the forest. Again, he paused, rewound, and magnified. He saw another man lifting a beartrap and sliding it into a bag. *Jesus!*

He played the footage through, and then replayed it. That was all he was getting—those two peculiar glimpses of the bastards of the Nucleus disarming. Feeling his heart accelerating, he reached into his pocket for his cell again and sought out the number of the stubborn butcher.

"Gordon?" Nicholas said. "I'm knee deep in ribs. Can I call you—"

"It's time."

"Time?" He paused. "How do you know?"

"The path has been cleared. I'll email you evidence. Start rallying the troops."

* * *

The back of Hardy's Conveniences was as weathered as the front. It only took Jake two shoulder barges to break the lock on the door.

"I'm surprised it's taken until now for someone to do that," Celestia said.

"Security hasn't been an issue on the streets of Mossbark for a long time due to your people."

Inside, Jake reached for the light switch but didn't press it just yet.

"I guess not," Celestia said. "Maybe I should have just repeated what my ancestors did? Offer that stability?"

"What? Pillage other towns to make this one happy? Close what's left of that back door, please."

Celestia obliged, and Jake hit the switch. The hallway illuminated, exposing two more doors. The one ahead was to the shop floor, and the one to the side was to the back office.

"I can't promise comfort," Jake said, heading down the hallway to the back office. "Was never invited back here." He put his hand on the handle and guffawed. "Did you know that the stubborn old bastard practically threw me out his shop the first time I met him!"

"I'm sorry about your friend. I'm sorry about what my people did to him."

"Thanks. But if there was ever a man who didn't want pity, Albert was that man." He opened the door.

The office was immaculately kept but had little floor

space. It was actually quite impressive how much Albert had managed to squeeze in.

"You can take the sofa." Jake pointed at a rickety office chair beside a desktop. "That'll do me."

"Nonsense," Celestia said from behind him. "That'll collapse under your weight! I'll head into the shop and find some blankets for the floor. If I keep the light off, no one will know—"

"No." Jake reached around the door and felt, with relief, the key was in the lock. "You'll lock yourself in here until the morning, and then we're getting out of here—out of Brady Crossing and out of Mossbark County. I've got enough money to keep us going. If you keep this locked, I'll sleep between the aisles on the shopfloor. Okay?"

She considered it and sighed. "Okay."

"Now, head in and hunker down." He sidestepped to let Celestia pass. "Close and lock the door. I'll be back in a minute."

Celestia turned. "Why?"

"Please?"

She closed the door, and he waited for the clunk of the key in the lock. He turned and approached the door to the shopfloor. He didn't expect danger but hesitated when he gripped the handle, knowing that seeing a shopfloor bereft of life and activity might aggravate the sense of loss burning inside Jake. After all, this shopfloor was Albert Hardy's world, and he had fought to keep it, warts and all, when the Nucleus's rotten money had poured into Brady Crossing and he'd refused any part of it.

To survive that storm, for so long, had been testament to the man.

Jake opened the door. The sun was setting, making the shopfloor dimly lit, so he used it to his advantage, skulking past aisles in this innocent little hollow Albert had carved out for himself in this rotten world. Jake went straight for the cash register and reached underneath the counter to grab the shotgun he knew Albert had stashed there. "You may be down, old man, but you've still got my back."

After exiting the shopfloor and carefully closing the door behind him, he knocked on the office door. "It's me."

Celestia opened the door. Her eyes widened when she saw the shotgun in his hands.

"Have you seen *Panic Room*?" Jake asked.

"Of course."

"This isn't *Panic Room*. This place is far from secure. This office door is like paper." He handed her the shotgun. "Anyone comes through it, use it. I won't be long. Oh, and take this." He reached into his pocket for his cellphone and handed that to her too. "I see a phone charger hanging from that USB over on that desktop. Could you get it charged please? We may need it. Now, lock me out again."

"Where're you going this time?"

"To break into a motel room with no security and retrieve my money from behind a wardrobe; it won't be an issue." He waited for the clunk of the lock. "At least I *hope* so."

12

When Jake arrived at the motel parking lot, he couldn't believe how unlucky he was. There were eleven motel rooms, and the only one with a window glowing was his old room. It hadn't been left on by mistake either. A single vehicle was in the lot, parked in that room's allotted space.

There went the smash and grab.

Once the sun had completely set, Jake headed through the parking lot. He glanced up at the security camera but wasn't too concerned. With one guest, he doubted it was even on. Additionally, he couldn't care less about being recorded on camera, because both him and Celestia would have skipped town before sunrise.

When he reached the motel room door, he gave it a gentle tap, stepped backward, and prepared to launch when it came ajar. He had no patience for a gentler approach. Revealing money was taped to the back of the wardrobe could end badly, nor did he have a weapon to negotiate with having handed the shotgun to Celestia.

The door started to come ajar. He tensed his legs, preparing himself.

An elderly woman's face peered out.

Jake stilled, exhaling slowly.

She opened the door and squinted through her glasses as she eyed him up and down.

"Who is it?" a croaky male voice came from within the room.

"I don't know, Bryan." The old woman continued to squint. "Who're you?"

The woman must be past eighty, and Jake felt dreadful for what was about to happen, but he had little choice. "Room service, ma'am?" he chanced, realizing immediately it was ridiculous. It was a cheap motel.

The woman eyed him up and down one more time and started to close the door.

Shit! Of all the situations ... He put the palm of his hand on the door so she couldn't close it. "Sorry, but—"

"*Bryan,*" she said, her face suddenly pale.

Jake didn't have to push himself hard to gain access. If anything, he held back, extremely concerned about knocking her over. He managed to slip inside and close the door behind him.

"What's the meaning of this, son?" Bryan was already on his feet.

"There's nothing to worry about," Jake said. "Seriously. I stayed here once and left something. I'm just here for it, and then I'm out of your hair." He saw tears in the elderly woman's eyes as she backed away from him. He felt his insides melting. "You have my word. I'm one of the good guys. Honest."

He spied her elderly husband hobble to the chair beneath the window and rustle through his clothing. It suddenly dawned on him what Bryan was probably doing—

Too late. The man was pointing a gun in his direction.

"There really isn't a need for that." Jake showed the palms of his hands. "Let me get what I came here for. I'll give you something for your troubles."

The elderly man's hands were shaking. The gun was *moving*.

"Okay, I understand," Jake said, annoyed with himself for letting those guilty moments dull his usual instincts. "I'll go."

"Now!" The old man's hands shook hard. The gun *waved* all over.

Jake reached to his side for the doorhandle—

The gun fired.

* * *

Celestia lapped the tiny office. Occasionally, she'd pause at the desktop, wondering if she should stream a movie. Ever since she could remember, classic movies were her go-to when her mind was troubled.

Troubled! She guffawed. *Try tormented!*

Inside such a tormented mind, it was inevitable, really, that the ghosts would eventually speak up.

Not so easy, my acorn, was it?

Not now, Father, she thought, pacing faster. *Please not now*.

You judged me for the decisions I made, and yet, here you are.

She paused at the sofa and stared down at it. Maybe if she lay down for a while, closed her eyes, the gods of sleep may just take mercy on this delirious young woman.

You watched them slaughter me, my acorn.

I didn't have a choice! She paced and paced.

You couldn't even forgive me in that final moment. It was the least you could have done. I loved you more than anything.

What you did, Father, was unforgivable.

Yet, here you are, basking in the very same failure.

At least I tried to do it the right way. She stopped at the desktop and hit the keyboard, killing the screensaver.

He grunted. The noise was *so* familiar. As a child, he'd do it regularly—often when she was telling white lies about the reasons she was late from curfew.

Tell me again your definition of the right way, my acorn?

Peace, Father. An end to conflict. An end to pain and suffering.

That familiar grunt again. *An end to sacrifice?*

What do you mean?

I mean, where's the man who owns this store? Where's Albert Hardy? Sacrificed by those who will never have peace. It seems you made the wrong decision, my sweet, gentle, little acorn …

Jake's cellphone, which she'd plugged in and laid by the keyboard, had now received enough charge to flare into life.

At least I never walked away. At least I tried to lead.

They killed you, Father. You never had an opportunity to walk away.

Jake's cellphone beeped. She noticed he had fifteen unread messages. She pressed one of the buttons, but it requested a passcode.

Chaos rages through the core. Because of you, Corrie will lead them all into destruction. Because of you, my acorn.

Tears welled in her eyes, and she let the mouse pointer

hover over the Internet Explorer icon. What movie could help free her turbulent mind?

You think you can be distracted from guilt, my acorn? Guilt is the ultimate consumer. Watch away, but you cannot forget how you left your people to the mercy of Corrie and Everlyn.

They made their choice. Did you hear them? The way they called for Albert's death?

Another grunt. *Fear, my acorn, fear makes people do awful things. What do you think will happen to all your people now? All those children?*

I can't think about. There's nothing I can do, Father.

Spoken like a true leader. I see that in our time together, I taught you nothing.

You taught me how not to be!

Maybe. But I taught you how to love your kind. Running away is not love, my acorn. It is cowardice.

So, what are you suggesting, Merithew? What would you do?

You know exactly what I'd do.

And she did. She *really* did. She felt adrenaline surge through her body. She moved the mouse pointer to the Word symbol and double clicked.

With trembling hands, she typed: *Dear Jake.*

With tears in her eyes, she typed: *I'm sorry.*

With rage ripping through her, she typed: *It's up to me. There is no one else.*

She heard a gunshot, followed by a smashing sound. *Albert's front window.* She backed away from the keyboard and reached for the shotgun.

* * *

"The next bullet won't miss," Bryan said.

Jake turned to look at the bullet hole in the wall, then back at the elderly man with the unsteady hands. *It probably will.* However, charging in would inflame the situation further. The whole thing was better off diffused.

"Bryan ..." Jake nodded at him, then his wife. "And your name is?"

"None of your goddamned business," Bryan said. "Eyes on me."

Jake inwardly sighed. "Okay, Bryan and wife, I'm here for one thing only. It'll be worth your while. Everything I own is behind that closet. Let me get my money, I'll give you a sizable chunk for inconveniencing you during your vacation, then I'll be on my way. What do you say?"

"I say that sounds like bullshit."

"Well, what does it matter? You have the gun. I'm unarmed. You might as well see if I'm telling the truth. It's in your best interests to trust me. It really is."

Despite shaking, the man appeared to be growing in confidence. He held his shoulders back as he aimed the gun, and a smarmy drawl had coated his voice. "If what you say is true. I could throw you out and take the money myself. Or better still ..." He nodded at the gun in his trembling hands.

"Bryan!" his wife said. "I can't believe—"

"This is not the time, Emily!" He looked at her nervously.

Emily narrowed her eyes at him, then faced Jake. She stepped in his direction. "Throwing you out might be a good thing though, young man."

"Listen," Jake said, addressing Emily now. "If I leave without that money, there'll be some very unhappy men. They'll come back, and they won't be as gracious as me."

"Drug money?" Bryan asked. "You do look the type."

"No," Jake lied, knowing it was highly likely this money *was* connected to drugs. At least back in the UK.

"Let him get his money," Emily said to her husband. "The problem isn't going away."

"I can make the problem go away—"

"*Bryan!* I will not tell you again. Get your money, stranger."

Jake nodded in gratitude and approached the closet. Using his big hands on the side closest to him, he started to work it out, hoping, *praying,* it would still be there. He'd never planned to leave it here for such a long time, but he'd been focused on looking after Celestia. He remained confident. He doubted the cleaners were ever dragging out the closet and cleaning behind it.

Once he pulled out the closet, he stepped around the side and saw, with some relief, that the duffel bag was sitting there, looking squashed and misshapen.

He knelt, dragged it free, and brushed off the dust. He unzipped it, rummaged through the tied bundles of notes, and chose a particularly thick one. He zipped the bag, stood, and offered the money to Emily.

Emily stepped forward.

"If you touch my wife, I shoot," Bryan said.

Jake held up the money and placed it slowly into Emily's hand.

She looked at them. "These aren't dollars."

"No. British pounds. You can convert them at the bank."

"How much is here?"

"Must be over a thousand dollars. It'll add gloss to your vacation."

Emily nodded. "Okay."

"Vacation!" Bryan said. "*Here?*"

"Passing through, then?" Not really wanting to engage, despite feeling guilty about swaggering in and disturbing their peace, Jake started for the exit with his bag over his shoulder.

"Not as such, no," Bryan said, keeping the gun on Jake.

Jake put his hand on the doorhandle but felt the sudden pull of curiosity. He inwardly sighed and watched Bryan lower his gun. "Why come to Brady Crossing, then?"

"Our son," Emily said from behind him. "Our son is missing."

"Your son?" Jake asked.

"Yes, apparently so."

"I'm sorry to hear that. Any idea what happened?"

"No ... He's always been an odd one, but this takes the cake. He just left his rig and ran off."

Jake felt a cold sensation start up his stomach. He released the handle. "Sorry ... a rig?"

"Yes, he's a truck driver."

The cold sensation spread through his veins.

"He's not been right for a long time," Emily said. "Not since he was widowed."

Jake steadied himself at the door, worried he was turning to ice. "What's his name?"

"Logan," Bryan said. "Logan Reed."

13

Gordon opened his door to a tall, suited man with gelled hair and a streak of white in his quiff. He was holding a badge, but Gordon didn't have a hope in hell of reading it with the amount of alcohol currently in his bloodstream.

"I'm Lieutenant Kevin Sullivan. Are you Sheriff Gordon Kane?"

Gordon leaned forward toward the badge, squinting, trying his best to confirm this through his alcoholic haze. He felt a bolt of adrenaline when he saw that Kevin was Maine State Police.

Jesus! A fucking stormtrooper at my house!

"And with a dead body in the back," Sarah called out. "You're royally fucked now."

Gordon bit his lip to stop himself from answering his wife. In his current predicament, rambling at the voices in his head wouldn't stand him in good stead.

"Can I help you, Lieutenant?"

Kevin tucked his belt into the inside pocket of his suit. "I'm sorry for the unexpected visit, Sheriff."

"Yes, it's unexpected. I didn't know MSP made house calls to the local sheriff?"

"They don't," Susan said. "Unless the sheriff is bent. So they know, you stupid shit stain! They know you're bent. And they'll soon know you're a murderer too!"

Gordon shook his head.

"Are you okay?" Kevin asked.

"Yes, I'm fine."

"Have you been drinking?"

"Yes, but I'm off duty. I assume that's okay?"

"Of course, Sheriff. I just wanted to ensure you weren't agitated."

"Anything but. I only drink the finest. It keeps the nerves calm."

"I hear where you're coming from there. I'm partial to Old Forester myself."

"Like a fucking sniffer dog, isn't he? All over you ..." Susan said.

"I'm sorry to come to your home, Sheriff, while you are off duty, but I needed to speak to you rather urgently. No one was at your office."

"My deputy's supposed to be there."

Kevin shook his head, smiling.

"I see. But was it necessary this evening, Lieutenant? I'll be available at work in the morning—"

"It's necessary, I'm afraid, Sheriff. I wish it wasn't. Believe me. They've just called me back from vacation for this one. I was hunting over seventy clicks away in East-holme, but that still made me the closest, and needs must, I suppose. You'll know that better than anyone."

"The job demands."

"A lieutenant called in off vacation!" Susan said.

"Christ, what do they have on you? Jesus! I could sell tickets for this!"

Get the fuck out of my head, woman!

"Are you sure you're okay, Sheriff? I need to come in and talk to you, and it'd be better if you weren't agitated."

"I'll be honest ... it's not a good time now. I've had a lot to drink, and I—"

"It's really not that simple, Sheriff, I'm afraid. I *still* need to talk to you as a matter of urgency. If you're too agitated to do it here, it will have to be at the office."

"Game. Set. Match," Susan said and laughed. "I'm *so* glad you kept me around. I wouldn't have missed this for the world."

"Come in. I'm fine." Gordon stepped back from the door, allowing him space to enter.

"Shall I take off my shoes?"

"Yes!" Susan said.

"No need," Gordon said.

"You always were a greasy toad, husband."

Kevin wandered into the lounge. "Jeez ... what's that smell?"

"Me!" Susan said.

"The trash," Gordon said. "I haven't put it out ... in a while."

Kevin looked around, grimacing.

"He thinks this place is a fucking pigsty," Susan said. "I keep telling you to clean up."

Kevin stepped over a mound of dirty clothing, which had yet found its way into the laundry room. He glanced at a pile of used crockery on the coffee table, then looked right into the kitchen, where more dirty dishes were on full view.

"My wife just left me." He thought it best to offer some reason for the smell and the chaos. "I mean, it wasn't that I left all the cleaning to my wife. It's just I've been down, you know? Down and neglectful."

Kevin turned. "You may want to do something about the smell."

"Yes ... You're right. I've started to get used to it. I barely notice it anymore." Gordon eyed the two doors—the one to the office and the one to their bedroom. Part of the smell was most certainly attributable to the trash and the rotten food, but part of it was down to his wife. He had tried everything he could to keep the smell down. He'd pulled the bed to the open window. As of yesterday, he'd started to lay tarpaulin over her. He used draft stoppers beneath the door and plug-in air-fresheners, but he was fighting a losing battle. He'd have to get rid of the body soon.

"Would you like to sit?" Gordon asked.

"Thank you." Kevin sat on the sofa and pulled a notepad from his suit pocket.

"How long?" Sarah asked. "How long before he sees through that rotting bin lie of yours? Look at his face! He's no mug! He'll put two and two together soon enough."

While Kevin perused his notes, Gordon tapped himself on the back of his head. *Just shut the fuck up, woman. How can I be expected to think with you in there?*

Kevin looked up as if he'd heard something.

Impossible, Gordon thought.

Kevin narrowed his eyes. "Are you going to sit too, Sheriff?"

"Would you like a drink first?"

"I'm good, thanks."

"Lucky for you," Sarah said. "He has a drink ... then what? He needs to take a piss."

Gordon's blood ran cold.

"Ha! You hadn't thought about that, had you?" Sarah said.

He lifted his eyes to the bedroom door. Their cottage only had one toilet, and it was through there.

"Should have taken up his offer to go to the office when you had the chance," Sarah said. "Can you see it unraveling? I can. God, I love watching you flounder."

With his heart thrashing in his chest, Gordon turned quickly from Kevin and moved into the kitchen. Sarah's laughter was booming in his head. He swooped for the bottle of whiskey, poured himself a tumbler, and gulped it back without pause. He put it down on the side and waited for the burning to subside. He also waited for that bitch's niggling voice again. It didn't come. He sighed and turned.

Kevin had left the sofa and was now standing opposite him in the kitchen. "Are you okay, Sheriff?"

"Yes ..."

Kevin nodded at the bottle of whiskey.

"Like I said, life has dealt me a tough hand recently. Look, maybe it's best we go to the office, after all. If anything, I could do with the fresh air—"

"We've had an anonymous report, Sheriff."

"Anonymous report?"

"A concerning one. Someone called to make accusations."

"Accusations?"

"Yes ... against you."

"Really? I mean? What about? Seriously?"

Sarah's laughter raged.

"We have a report stating someone died in your custody."

Gordon widened his eyes. "Died?"

"Yes."

"Who?"

"Someone called Walker. He comes from a group of travelers who reside in the hills."

"Travelers in the hills! Don't make that mistake. They're not travelers. They live there, *fester* there. Have for as long as anyone can remember."

"Well, nomadic or not, the caller said a man from this community was in your custody, and he died."

Gordon laughed. "I've never heard anything so ridiculous."

"Well, like I said, the caller was vague on the details, but my superiors considered it interesting enough to pull me from my vacation."

"I can only imagine how pissed you must be."

"Well ... the point is—"

"Especially with this being such a goddamned waste of time!"

"Who's Walker?"

"Honestly, I've no idea."

"I've checked your arrest records."

"And?"

"No Walker."

"Precisely, because I've never come across Walker before. Are you sure this tip was about me? The Mossbark Sheriff? I mean, there are a lot of sheriffs in these parts."

Kevin nodded and referred to the notebook in his hand. "Gordon Kane, Sheriff of Mossbark County. They were fairly detailed in that regard. Not so detailed about the death, unfortunately, and the reasons for it."

"Because it didn't happen—not here, at any rate." Gordon sighed and held up his hands. "Look, I concede that I'm not in the best state. I'm living in squalor and drinking

136

way too much. But I don't drink at work, and I run a tight ship. Have you checked my history?"

"Yes."

"And?"

Kevin smirked. "Well, you wouldn't have drawn attention to it if there was any dirt, would you?"

"This whole thing is unsubstantiated bullshit, *and* that's not the liquor talking."

"Could be. Although, I like to be a little bit more thorough in my check. Don't want to end up being pulled away from my vacation again, do I?"

"Well, there won't be any danger of that, I can assure you. Shall we head to the office and put your mind at rest?"

"Best way. I'm assuming the caller is referring to your jail cell, so I think giving you the all-clear there is key."

"You better hope Scott did a good job with that mop!" Susan said.

Jesus! Is there any shutting you up!

Kevin nodded at the bottle. "I'll drive you. Also, I just did seventy clicks and am bursting. Where's your bathroom?"

Gordon opened his mouth to respond, but he was suddenly drowning in the sound of his wife's laughter and couldn't speak.

* * *

Celestia couldn't help herself; she was desperate to know who had caved in Albert's shop window. Armed with a shotgun, she unlocked the office room, crept down the hallway, and went through onto the shopfloor. She heard another shop window smash outside and heard voices. She slipped down the aisle, crouched, and peered through the broken window. She gulped.

Fern, Ibre, and Glynnie stalked Main Street.

The muscle of the Nucleus.

Unlike typical rioters—swollen with anger, bloodlust, and sometimes greed—these three moved slowly and thoughtfully. They paused at each shopfront, possibly admiring the impressive front window displays that the Nucleus had funded. Then one of them would raise a shotgun and decimate it.

Bang!

It was trading hours, so Celestia assumed, *hoped*, the storeowners had taken cover in much the same way that she, herself, was hunkered behind a display of household cleaning products. She tightened her grip on the shotgun Jake had given her. Maybe now was as good a time as any to take a stand against these traitors.

Corrie and Everlyn came into view. They were following their soldiers at some distance. Both had rifles over their backs, but their hands were thrust into their pockets. They didn't communicate with the soldiers or each other. They just stared dead ahead, orchestrating the uprising against Mossbark with their presence.

Everything Celestia hadn't wanted, everything she'd fought to avoid was playing out in front of her very eyes. *War.*

Feeling herself welling up, she forced back her emotion. There could be no time for tears. Maybe, just maybe, if she stayed strong, there could be an opportunity now in this unfolding horror. After all, the threat within the borders of the Nucleus was *here* and not *there*.

Which meant, just possibly, if she were to return home at this moment, she could get control of her people again. It was a long shot, she knew. What she'd seen at Albert's execution had shaken her to the very core, but maybe their support for Corrie, in that moment, had simply been born from great fear? In Corrie's absence, would they swing back to Celestia's side?

She had to try.

After everything her father had done, she owed her people that much.

She left the soldiers on their path of destruction, exited the store through the back door, and made for the Nucleus.

14

The office door was locked. Jake pounded on it and waited.

No answer.

With his good friend Logan missing, he wasn't to be deterred. He went at the door harder this time. "Open the fucking door!"

Eventually, the door did open.

Scott said, "I thought you were part of the core now?"

"Where's the sheriff?"

"Don't know," Scott said. "The office is closed."

"You need to open. Logan Reed is missing."

Jake expected a dismissive retort—at the very least, a sneer—but he didn't get either, which was very out of character. Scott seemed distracted and, as a result, less antagonistic than usual.

"We know," Scott said. "He ran away. Parked his rig and sprinted into the unknown."

"How do you know?"

"Someone saw, obviously."

"Who?"

"Not relevant to you," Scott said. "He ran. He'll be back. We aren't going to put manpower on someone having a nervous breakdown."

"A familiar theme, eh?" Jake narrowed his eyes. "Not putting any manpower on it? I'm not sure why you'd ever bother to reopen this office! None of you seem in any way bothered about doing the job!"

"Logan Reed is not a victim. Get over it."

"He's a missing person. Have you explained to his parents that you aren't bothering? They're in town. They probably came to see you, but your door was closed; this is a joke shop."

"Why the concern anyway, Frank? Aren't you one of the hillbillies now? Shouldn't you be hunting dinner or gathering firewood?"

"Well, you'd know, sending your drones over, peeping in. I bet it was you who came sneaking in through the woods earlier too."

Scott avoided eye contact.

"Jesus," Jake said. "It was, wasn't it? Sneaking in like thieves! You're the police, for pity's sake! I don't think I've ever seen anything so pathetic."

"We lack manpower. You can count us on one hand! How else are we supposed to shut down the Nucleus?"

"Why the sudden need to shut them down anyway?" Jake said. "You've been content to let them be for several hundred years—"

"They're a cancer. Always have been. Always will be."

"Like I said, seems quite late in the day to start caring about that now."

"They're filthy killers. And you know that, Frank. You're only lingering because you've got yourself all hot and bothered over one of them. Isn't she a little young for you?"

Jake clenched his fist. *Here he is. Antagonistic Scott is back, bold as brass, balls swinging.*

Scott smiled at Jake's fist. "Lookin' for a night in the cell, are you?"

"Where's Logan's rig?"

"Why?"

"Someone has got to try to figure out what's happened—"

A loud gunshot and the sound of smashing glass rang out.

"Shit," Scott said, reaching for his sidearm. "What the hell was—"

A second gunshot. More smashing glass.

"It's coming from Main Street."

Main Street. Hardy's Conveniences. Celestia. Jake felt his stomach contract.

"It's them, isn't it?" Scott asked, heading down the steps. "They're here."

Jake followed, adrenaline surging. "What did you expect? You moved on them first."

A third gunshot.

Jake and Scott started to run.

* * *

"Bathroom, please?" Kevin repeated for the third time.

Gordon gulped. "Yes ... of course ..."

"You might want to slow down on that." Kevin pointed to the bottle of whiskey.

Gordon thought his head might explode from his wife's laughter. He gritted his teeth, desperately trying to force her unpleasant cackle deep into his subconscious. It didn't work. "Out of order. The toilet ... I'm afraid."

"Your toilet is out of order?"

"Yes, it's not flushing."

"How can you live without a toilet?"

"Only happened today ... a short time before you arrived, actually ... was planning to call someone."

"If he didn't have enough doubts about you before, honey," Sarah said, "he must be absolutely riddled with them by now!"

Gordon gritted his teeth as hard as he could.

"Best thing is to let me take a look for you," Kevin said. "And if I can't get it flushing, I'll just pour some water in it after I go."

"Wow!" Sarah said. "Just give it up, Gordon. You're done! This is getting cringeworthy—"

"Shut the hell up!" Gordon shouted.

Kevin stepped away from him.

"No ... *sorry*. Not you," Gordon said, showing the palms of his hands.

Kevin looked to either side. "No one else's here, Sheriff."

"I know ... I know. You're right. I've had too much to drink. I just need to sit, perhaps. Shall we just go to the office now?"

Kevin creased his brow. "Where's your bathroom, Sheriff?"

"That's it," Sarah said. "You ramped up his suspicion levels to DEFCON One. Just show him. Put us all out of our misery. That's it ... lift your hand ... point."

Gordon was surprised to see he'd obeyed his wife's instruction and pointed at her bedroom door.

"In there?" Kevin said.

"Tell him yes. For the sake of everyone's sanity, Gordon, just tell him yes."

"Yes," Gordon said.

Kevin pointed at him. "Stay here, Sheriff." He turned toward the bedroom door.

As Kevin approached the bedroom door, Gordon scanned the room for ideas in a futile situation. Just prior to his wife's death, he'd put a new painting above the mantlepiece—a copy of Nighthawk by Edward Hopper; three people congregated in a New York diner, lost in their own thoughts.

New York. How he'd loved New York.

The picture itself gave him an idea—not the subject matter but rather the attachment of the painting to the wall.

He heard the bedroom door open.

The electric drill he'd used to puncture the walls for the painting still lay on the mantlepiece.

"Jesus," Kevin said. "The smell."

Gordon was already at the mantlepiece with the electric drill in hand. He turned to see Kevin enter the bedroom, holding his hand to his nose. His other hand was already fumbling for a sidearm.

"Too slow, old man," Sarah said.

Fuck you, Gordon thought and charged. *How's this for old?*

Kevin had started to turn, but Gordon, contrary to his wife's claim, still had the edge. He hit the tall MSP Trooper side on and sent him crashing to the carpet.

Gordon pressed his boot on Kevin's wrist so he was unable to maneuver his firearm.

"Get the hell off me!" Kevin shouted.

Gordon kicked the trooper's face. Then he quickly checked his torque was set to a hundred percent. He couldn't resist a smile in his wife's direction, despite the fact she was lost beneath the tarpaulin, then held down the trigger.

The electric drill hummed.

He leaned over and listened to the drill bit squeal as it burrowed into the side of Kevin's head. "You should never have come here," Gordon said.

"You and me both," Sarah said.

* * *

"I expected more from them," Everlyn said from alongside Corrie.

The lack of resistance, however, did not surprise Corrie. "Why? Think about how long they've been sheltering, how long *we've* sheltered them. They never needed to fight!"

The two leaders paused and watched Ibre fire into the record store window. The glass exploded. He whooped with delight and fired again.

Everlyn stepped forward. "Ibre, enough—"

Corrie put a hand on Everlyn's shoulder. "*No.* It's our time. Let him be. Let them enjoy it."

Everlyn looked her in the eyes, paused, then nodded in agreement.

The next shop along had a colorful display of boxes in the window and an arrangement of contraptions Corrie was unfamiliar with. She read the sign: Mossbark Vapor Worx. She looked at Everlyn, who explained the concept of vaping.

"The world has moved on in peculiar ways," Corrie said. "I don't envy the regular visits you had to make here—"

Glynnie fired into the storefront, decimating the display of contraptions. Being a slight woman, the force from the shotgun jolted her backward.

"You want me to hold your hand next time?" Ibre asked.

"Last thing you'll ever fucking do—"

Another gunshot sounded, and Glynnie again recoiled backward. This time, she didn't stop, and when she landed on her back, twitching, it was clear her weapon's kickback hadn't caused it. Someone had shot her from within the shop.

"Take cover!" Ibre shouted.

The three surviving soldiers pinned themselves to the wall between stores and crouched, rifles at the ready.

Corrie remained in the center of Main Street, watching the motionless Glynnie as a pool of blood grew around her.

"Get the fuck down, Corrie!" Everlyn hissed.

Corrie approached the broken window. She didn't even bother to ready her rifle and simply let it bounce off her back. She stopped opposite the gaping hole in the front of Mossbark Vapor Worx. "I'm the leader here—"

Another gunshot made Corrie flinch, then she smiled. She eyed Everlyn, who was shaking her head and mouthing, *What the hell are you doing?*

"The next one is in your head," a grizzled voice called from inside.

"That would be a mistake, and you know it. Hence the reason I'm still standing," Corrie said. "Shoot me, you start a war."

"You're the ones here starting the goddamned war!"

"No. You came to us first. Through our woods. You killed two of our people."

"What the hell are you talking about?"

"I'm talking about retaliation. And you, Mr. Mossbark Vapor Worx, can end this standoff any time you see fit. Come out and lay down your weapon. And I'll show you our more diplomatic side."

"Ha!" Another gunshot.

Expecting it, Corrie did not flinch this time.

"Diplomatic, my ass. You're savages!"

Corrie laughed. She noticed Everlyn, Ibre, and Fern were still crouching, taking cover, watching her incredulously. She didn't bother trying to decipher what Everlyn was mouthing to her this time.

"I see you have made your decision, Mr. Worx—"

"It's Reeves. *John* Reeves. Use my name, savage. Use it, or I will blow a hole in your head."

"Corrie!" Everlyn shouted.

"Shoot me, *John*," Corrie said. "Shoot me, I beg of you. Then watch the fire and fury roll down from the hills—"

"Wait!"

Corrie snapped her head right to see a tall policeman walking up Main Street with his hands raised. Corrie smiled. "You got lucky, John. The law is here."

"I got lucky!" John called from within. "You're the one standing in my fucking crosshairs!"

"John! Enough!" the officer said. Several feet from Corrie, he knelt on the ground and laid down his sidearm. "I'm Deputy Scott Derby, ma'am." He rose and held up his hands again.

Corrie smirked.

John shouted, "Are you suicidal, Scott?"

"I'm just here to stop this from getting out of control."

"Goddammit!" John replied. "It's already out of fucking control!"

Corrie stroked the strap across her chest. "So, tell me, Deputy, did you come alone?"

Scott took a deep breath as the color drained from his face. "Yes."

"Brave boy."

"Stupid boy is what he is," John said. "Fortunately, for you, Scott, if she reaches for that rifle, it'll be the last thing she ever does."

"It's okay." Scott turned a palm toward the shop window. "Just put down your weapon, John, and come out. I got this—"

"What the absolute fuck have you been drinking?" John asked.

Corrie gestured for the three crouching soldiers between the stores to stand. "But keep your weapons down, soldiers. Let's not get ourselves into a Mexican standoff."

Everlyn and the others joined her and, as instructed, kept their weapons lowered.

"Ha! Give the word, Scott," John said. "I only need one stone for these four birds. They picked the wrong shop today."

"Please be quiet, John!" Scott said.

Corrie nodded toward the shop. "He's a confident buck, ain't he?"

"Ma'am," Scott said, "please head back to your vehicle, which I'm assuming is parked that way." Scott pointed down Main Street past the wrecked storefronts. "And go back into the hills. We need to let this settle. When everyone is calm, we can talk. It's time to put this whole situation to rest—"

"Tell me, Deputy," Corrie said, "were you one of the men who came into our back yard earlier?"

Scott flinched. "I ..."

"Did you?"

"I—"

"Silly boy."

"Yes. It was a mistake."

Corrie raised her eyebrows at Everlyn. "It took the little boy until now to realize this!"

"Fuck you! I lost my brother because of your hellhole."

Corrie tilted her head to the side. *Interesting.* "Your brother? Was that the boy we shot?"

"No, that was Riley," Scott said. "Brad was caught in one of your traps. We carried him back, but he lost too much blood. Both *were* deputies, ma'am. You must see what trouble you're in. It's best we just put an end to this now."

"How unfortunate for you, eh? Were you and your brother close?"

"We were twins. Listen, we've all made mistakes ... awful mistakes ... but now is—"

"Mistakes!" Corrie smiled. "You think? Who was it that decided coming through our woods was a good idea?"

"The sheriff ... and I'm through with him. In fact, he's through!"

"Are you out of your motherfucking mind, Scott?" John said.

"Shut the hell up!" Scott said.

"You're reasoning with goddamned savages. Where the hell is Kane anyhow?" John asked. "We need a real voice of goddamned reason around here!"

"Drinking himself into oblivion," Scott hissed. "He's a mess. Has been for a while."

"From where I'm standing," John said, "you're the person in a mess—"

"*Shut up*! The both of you," Corrie said. "How's anybody supposed to think?"

"Please," Scott said. "This is your chance, *our* chance, to end it all. Let me handle it."

"Handle it how?" Corrie said.

"I told you he's through," Scott said. "The sheriff is out of the picture."

"How so? Have you killed him?"

"No, I have not!"

"Well, then we have a problem," Corrie said. "Because anything short of death won't stop a man willing to march through our woodland."

Scott shook his head. "No. Trust me, please. I'm putting an end to this—"

"I've three dead soldiers, Deputy. *Three. Dead. Soldiers.* Walker, Thaxton, and"—she looked down at the corpse at her feet—"Glynnie. How many are your side down, Deputy? Two? Your brother and the boy we shot ..."

A look of anger flashed over Scott's face. "I've lost my brother ... *my* little brother!"

"But still. Three to two still seems a little unfair, don't you think?"

"I'm happy to make it seven/two, bitch," John said.

"You won't get that far," Corrie said through the broken window. "Besides, it's actually three apiece now, so steady your hands."

"Sorry?" Scott said.

"This is very honest of me." Corrie looked at Everlyn. "Albert Hardy. I gutted him back in the Nucleus." She enjoyed watching the young deputy pale again.

He opened his mouth to speak, but it took him a while to get out, "Why?"

"It's a long story. Point is, he shouldn't have been there." She ran a hand over her shaven head. "On second thoughts, I'm not classing him as number three, because he wasn't really one of your soldiers. So, that, I'm afraid, means we're not even after all." She turned and looked between Everlyn, Fern, and Ibre. She could see the anger in their faces.

They'd lost Glynnie. They were hurting. Again, she looked between them, then nodded at Ibre's weapon belt and raised her gaze to see the burly man's look of gratitude. Corrie turned back. "We even the score, then I'll accept your peace terms."

Scott shook his head. "How do we even the score? Me?" He started to back away. "Without me, there's no peace."

"No, be calm! Not you, Deputy." Corrie narrowed her eyes. "But you do have to do something for me right now. Something important."

"What?"

"Duck!" Corrie dropped onto Glynnie's body as Ibre's arm looped in the air, tossing his grenade into the shop.

She heard John shout, "Fuckers!" as his firearm discharged. Whether anyone was hit at this point, she couldn't tell, because her colleagues were all diving for cover anyway.

An explosion sounded deep within the shop, and although debris rained onto them, there wasn't much glass to bite into them, because the windows had been taken out before.

Scott lay face down on the floor, covering his head.

She noticed his firearm was a foot from him and was relieved when Everlyn darted from a crouching position to retrieve it. Knowing John's death was about to bring other terrified storeowners fleeing from their shops, potentially wielding weapons, it was time for a sharp exit. "We'll be in touch," Corrie hissed to the cowering deputy.

Scott didn't respond.

She stood and turned.

With her companions all uninjured and alive, apart from Glynnie, they followed her as she fled down Main Street toward their vehicle.

15

J ake had broken off from Scott on their approach to Main Street. The deputy was going at a heck of a pace, so had been none the wiser. Jake sprinted behind the stores on the left side of Main Street. When he reached Hardy's Conveniences, he entered through the back door he'd broken through earlier with Celestia.

His heart fell when he discovered the office door unlocked and the room empty.

He headed out of the office, down the hallway, through the door, and onto the shopfloor again. Outside, on Main Street, he heard loud voices but, thankfully, no more gunfire.

Other than the smashed window of a clothing store opposite, he could see little else from his position near the back of the shop, so he was forced against the broken glass to peer out and down Main Street.

Outside Mossbark Vapor Worx, Albert's killer, Corrie, was again holding court over proceedings. Scott, unusually bereft of his bravado, was disarmed with his hands in the air, and someone, potentially a victim, lay on the floor between them. Three of the Nucleus' soldiers stood with Corrie, and Jake surmised the deputy's short time on this earth could well be coming to end.

Attempting to save Deputy Scott's life—or anyone's in Mossbark, for that matter—was very low on Jake's list of priorities. Only one item graced that list.

Celestia.

He was about to turn from the window to resume his search when he heard Corrie warning everyone to duck as the larger of her soldiers hurled something through the window of Vapor Worx. Jake didn't dive to the ground, as it was covered in broken glass, but he did shield himself behind the closed shop door. After the explosion had shaken Main Street, Jake chanced another peek through the window to see Corrie and her three soldiers sprinting toward Hardy's Conveniences. He drew back his head again and listened as they charged past. He waited until he heard the rumble of a distant vehicle, indicating a possible departure, before turning for another look.

Flames billowed from Vapor Worx. Shop owners had poured forth from their premises, armed with fire extinguishers.

Jake wondered if the townsfolk would head into the Nucleus to end this war once and for all. Not that this was his fight anymore. He was done with the Nucleus. He was done with Mossbark. He was done with *everything*.

Apart from Celestia.

He returned to the empty office and gave it a once over. He was relieved that he couldn't find the shotgun. Wherever she was, at least she was armed.

A horrible thought entered his mind, and he slumped onto the office chair, tasting bile. *Had she gone back?* He shook his head. *She wouldn't be that stupid. Would she?* He slammed down his fist. His cellphone hopped clear, yanking out the USB cable, and the cell toppled down the side of the desk. The computer screen glowed into life, and he read the words on the open Word document.

Dear Jake,

I'm sorry.

It's up to me. There's no one else.

The message felt incomplete, as if she'd been interrupted. But Corrie and those soldiers hadn't found her. He'd just seen them out there on Main Street, so ...

Think, Jake ... goddammit ... what has she done?

He rubbed his temples, trying desperately to put himself in her shoes, trying to understand what a desperate young woman shouldering the burden of a dying community would have done when Corrie had brought war to Brady Crossing.

And then he had it.

No, no, no ... You planned to go back, but you saw them here, didn't you? You heard them! They distracted you as you wrote this message, then you watched them through the smashed glass in the same way I had done. You thought, now or never. You thought that while the soldiers were here, the Nucleus was wide open—wide open for you to sneak inside and head to Corrie's house. And you planned to ambush her. Her son Marston wouldn't be an obstacle. You could incapacitate him and kill Corrie in the same way you killed those elders. Then you could have taken back your soldiers and appeased them by allowing them to set up their defenses again. You could take back the Nucleus. Try again. Another go. Better luck this time. Except ... He stood up. *Except you're on foot! And they're heading back earlier than you anticipated! Oh, you impetuous girl! What if they see you?*

What if Corrie, God forbid, goes to her house before you arrive there?

Jake moved back from the table, his heart hammering in his chest—

His cellphone beeped. He knelt, reached down the side of the desk, and checked the screen. Fifteen unread messages. He opened them. All voicemail requests. He called voicemail. His latest message was from yesterday evening.

"Hey, partner. I know we said our goodbyes already, but I was just about to leave Mossbark, and, you know, this fat fool just got, well, kind of sentimental! I know you haven't got reception up there in that wilderness, but I figured you'd hear this message one day, and by that point, you'd be missing dear old Logan Reed. After all, never really had many friends, and out of the one or two I have had, I don't remember ever feeling about them the way I feel about you, brother. So ... I just wanted you to remember my offer is all. I don't want you forgetting about Yorke and Reed Motorcycles. You'll have to settle down some time. Wait ... just a minute. Seems I have company. Not a police cruiser, so I guess I'm not in trouble for parking on the road out of town and creating some almighty obstacle. Hang on, they're coming over. I'll call you back. That's funny. It's ..."

Jake listened to the name of the person who'd approached Logan's truck and tasted bile again. Then he dove for the duffel bag of money stored behind the sofa before exiting the office and the store at full tilt, pocketing his cellphone.

* * *

Gordon washed the blood splatter from his face and bagged his soiled shirt.

His wife had been silent for a while now. He wasn't sure if it was the murder of Lieutenant Kevin Sullivan that had caused the peace and quiet or the Hennessey, but Lord was he thankful for it!

He stared at the corpse, face down in a pool of blood, and pondered his next move. Of course, he could have a crack at disposing of the body and burning the evidence, but was there really any point? MSP would know he had come here before disappearing off the face of the earth—meaning he was, as Sarah had so eloquently put it earlier, *royally fucked*.

However, he wasn't breaking a sweat, and his heartbeat stayed steady. Yes, he was laced with whiskey, but that wasn't the reason he was nonchalant. He was nonchalant because nothing had really changed.

He'd already been royally fucked before this swinging dick from MSP had shown up.

The bodies had been mounting up for a while: three of those bastards from the Nucleus—Angelita, Walker, and some other knuckle-dragger in the forest—and two of his men, if Brad ended up kicking the bucket too. Throw in drunk Leo and his dead witch of a wife, Sarah, into the equation, and he must *surely* be close to that finishing line. And not to forget Scott ... his beloved Scott. It was he, the traitorous bastard, who'd only gone and invited MSP along to play!

No, that finishing line wasn't just close. It was *there*! Right in front of him, pressed against his chest as he started through it ...

His next move couldn't have been any more obvious.

He pulled his cellphone from his pocket and was just

about to hit the call button when it vibrated. He answered. "Jeez, Nicholas, I was just about to call—"

"He's dead. Raging is *fucking* dead!"

"Woah, Nicholas, calm down ... *calm down*! What's happened?"

"They came down to Main Street. The Nucleus *came* to Main Street. They killed Raging—"

"The Nucleus? Really? All of them?"

"No, five. They shot up the place. Raging managed to get one of them. Shot 'em stone cold. But they put a grenade through his store window. Blew the poor bastard to pieces. And then they ran. Back to where they'd crawled from."

"Wow," Gordon said.

"Is that all you have to say?"

"No, sorry, Nicholas. I'm just surprised. Stunned, actually. I didn't expect this ... no, I didn't expect this at all." He felt his heart up-tempo.

"Retaliation for what you've done, Sheriff," Nicholas said. "They said as such."

"No, Nicholas. Not at all. This isn't retaliation. This is a wild animal, cornered and scared. It just lashed out, yes, and poor old John Raging Reeves paid that price, but listen carefully, they know they're vulnerable." He took a deep breath and enjoyed the build-up of adrenaline in his system. "Posturing, pure and simple. They can't hold us out any longer, so they believe offense is the best form of defense. You know what this means, Nicholas?"

"Sheriff, everyone is shaken up. I don't think this is the time—"

"It's the most *perfect* time! How many do you have, Nicholas? How many people do we have to take back our land?"

"Now that Raging is gone, fifteen."

"Get them all to Main Street. Let them look at what the Nucleus has done. Remind them what our neighbors in the hills are capable of. I'll be there shortly."

"Okay. But, Sheriff, there is something else ..."

"Go on."

"Your deputy, Scott. He's here."

Gordon narrowed his eyes. "Understandable. There's been a crime—"

"No. He *was* also here when they were."

"Really? And did he not put up a fight?"

"Quite the opposite. He laid down his weapon and told them we were ready for peace."

Gordon took a deep breath.

"He also told them his brother was dead and that you were finished. Said you were in a mess. I heard it all."

So, he really had lost Scott. "And they believed him?"

"Yes ... of course ... I think so. Why wouldn't they?"

"Hope, Nicholas. *Hope.* And they will be even more vulnerable for it now."

"So, Scott was lying?"

"Of course. Get everyone ready, Nicholas. *Be ready.* I will be there soon."

He hung up and closed his eyes, enjoying the absence of his wife's incessant criticisms, feeling that finishing line pressed tight against his chest.

16

When Celestia reached the edge of the southernmost forest, she looked across the Focus and sighed. It was a place that would forever occupy her heart, no matter what was to unfold. She worked herself along the perimeter of the trees, gazing at the cabins and *into* her many joyous memories. The gardens planted and tended to by Gillie were as beautiful as ever. Celestia reminisced over the first time she'd asked Gillie if she could help tend the flowers with her—it'd been the first day of many long days together.

After bypassing the swaying rope swing that she'd hung with her closest friend, she recalled a time when her father, Merithew, had admonished her for straying too far into the woods, where many dangerous traps were set to protect them from intruders.

She took a deep breath and forced herself to acknowledge how much she'd loved that man. And again, as always, the realization of what he had become in the years before his death ripped her heart to pieces.

She drew level with Corrie's cabin. She narrowed her

eyes as she stared at her destination. "The world has too many tyrants," she said, before breaking cover and sprinting across the grassy area.

Catching her breath beside her destination, she looked skyward, imagining her father watching over her. *If you want to make up for what you did. Help me now.* The clouds parted, and a shaft of sunlight broke loose and illuminated the Focus around her. It seemed too empty in the residential area, too quiet.

Is this your doing, Father? Have you cleared my way? She smirked. *Nah.*

Here was the reality; she'd just been sprinting in the open for twenty seconds or so, and someone probably had seen her. Add to that, Corrie could very well be home now or, at the very least, her son.

No. Her dead father was not offering a protective veil. It was quiet in the Focus, because most people would be in the square, socializing and trading. So she'd just have to hope that if someone had seen her, they'd be a sympathizer and see Celestia as true leader—a leader who loved them more than could be imagined. The observer may just offer Celestia their silent complicity.

She glanced again at the closed cabin door beside her and tried to listen for some tell-tale signs of occupancy. But the Focus and the cabin were silent, and all she could hear was her heart thrashing in her chest. She checked the shotgun in her hands. It was now or never.

For Gillie. For my father—or, at least, the man he once was. For Thaxton. And for everyone betrayed in our community ...

She leaned over, pressed the cabin doorhandle, gave it a little push, and let it glide open. She turned into the doorway, shotgun in both hands, and almost pulled the trigger when she saw the figure hunched over a table at the back of the room. When her eyes adjusted to the gloom and she saw who it was, she sighed with relief.

"Marston?"

He didn't look up and was busy writing or drawing.

"Marston ... is your mother home?" she asked in a hush whisper, which was rather irrelevant. If Corrie was in this cabin, she'd certainly be aware of Celestia's presence.

Keeping the shotgun in one hand, Celestia gently closed the cabin door behind her. The room was dim due to all the curtains being drawn and the lights being off, but her young eyes adjusted, and the shadows around her quickly sharpened into identifiable shapes.

The cabin was organized like most cabins in the Focus. A large kitchen area was outfitted with only the essentials, such as cutlery, pans, and chopping boards, and two doors alongside the right side of the room led to sleeping areas.

Celestia, maneuvering her shotgun around the cabin until she was certain no one was skulking in the shadows, approached the boy. "Is anyone else home, Marston?"

No reply. He seemed completely lost to whatever he was creating on that table.

As she drew closer, the boy hunched over farther, and Celestia wondered if he were cowering from her. However, she continued, and a yard or so from him, she noticed the real reason he'd folded farther over was to put more weight into the crayon he was scribbling with. "Marston?"

When he didn't respond, she determined this was the last time she would gently try for his attention and closed the gap to the boy. She eyed the drawing—or, at least, what *remained* of the drawing. He was currently demolishing it with a red crayon. The image was of figures lying on the floor—bloody corpses, she assumed, because this was where

Marston was copiously applying the red crayon. Between the two bodies stood a tall woman holding a knife. *Corrie?* Could the two victims be Marston's father, Sumner, and his grandfather, Albert?

"You poor child …" Celestia took one hand from the shotgun to place it on his shoulder. She felt the muscles in his shoulder twitch as he worked the crayon. "Marston, I need you to listen to me. I need your help."

He worked the crayon harder.

She felt his muscles spasm again. "Your mother has betrayed your family … betrayed you."

The crayon snapped in two. He let the pieces fall from his hand.

"It's not safe for you—"

Clank.

She pulled her hand from Marston's shoulder and faced the bedroom doors. With both hands again, she waved the shotgun between the two closed rooms.

Clank.

Her stomach turned upside down.

Clank.

"Marston, who's in *there*? Is it your mother?"

Unsurprisingly, no reply came from the boy behind her.

Clank.

"*Who's* in there?"

Clank. Clank. Clank.

It sounded like someone was trapped, trying to get out of something. The clanking was continuous now. She spoke loudly above it. "I have a shotgun." Carefully, Celestia approached the first door on the left, pinned her ear against it, and realized immediately the source of the clanking was from the adjacent room. She took a deep breath and pointed the shotgun at the right door, wondering if her best option was to blow a hole in it.

Stupid and impetuous, she thought, feeling the adrenaline coursing through her. *Blow a hole in whoever is behind it. And if it's not Corrie you slaughter, then ... way to go, Celestia! Fuck.*

She took her other hand from the shotgun and pressed the handle. She recalled the game of Russian roulette that had ended Nick's life in *The Deer Hunter*. She felt like she had the gun pressed to her temple right now—

She kicked the door open, while simultaneously dragging her hand back to the shotgun.

In such a small room, she could identify the source of the clanking immediately and knew there was no Corrie and, at this exact moment, no danger. However, even though the feeling of having a gun to her temple may have waned, a sense of shock was now upon her.

A small animal cage had been pushed into the corner of the room. A small man was squashed inside, with just enough space to kick out at the bars and make that clanging sound which had brought Celestia to him.

She entered the room and recognized him. "Logan?"

He made a muffled sound, and she noticed the tape binding his mouth shut.

She approached the cage, placed the shotgun on top of it, and knelt so she was level with the truck driver.

He'd managed to get himself into a sitting position despite the limited space. His hands were tied behind his back, and he had a wound on his temple and dried blood on his cheek.

She ran her hands down the front of the cage until it reached the padlock. "Shit."

* * *

Marston had enjoyed the feel of Celestia's hand on his shoulder—a *genuine* touch, one full of warmth and concern, one he hadn't felt for a long time, one he'd never expected to feel again. He turned over the paper and, using a pencil, quickly sketched himself. He made himself stand tall without the weight that always pressed him down now.

Behind him, as Logan kicked at his cage, Marston listened to Celestia call out to the bedrooms. "Who's in there?"

Celestia, daughter of Merithew.

Merithew. The man who'd guided him toward love, toward Brittany Hirst.

Brittany. Hirst. A forbidden love—a love so wrong it'd been cut out of his heart as if it were a tumor.

Thank you, Merithew. Thank you for that legacy of pain.

I owe you.

He started on the second image, a prone figure on the floor. Behind him, he heard Celestia open the bedroom door and soon after gasped. "Logan?"

Realizing he'd forgotten to sketch a knife in his self-image, Marston rectified that now. Then he reached for the broken red crayon and dug it deep into the image of Celestia at his feet until she, as his father and grandfather had been moments before, was completely covered.

It's time to settle up, Merithew.

17

Before traveling too deeply into the southernmost forest, Jake remembered that Logan's message hadn't been the only voicemail. There'd been *considerably* more. Fourteen, in fact.

After discovering that Marston had taken Logan, combined with his prediction that Celestia was journeying to that boy's cabin this very moment, which had been one hell of a distraction, he was now heading back into those dark hills; curiosity had reared its head and bitten deep. He would soon be losing all reception on this cellphone—potentially forever. A cat had to run out of lives eventually.

Fourteen messages were lot of messages to never hear, especially with a young child. So, he listened. Afterward, he felt the ground giving way beneath him but managed to lean against a tree. It didn't stop the contents of his stomach coming up though.

After he wiped his mouth, he held the cellphone with his trembling hand and searched for Michael Yorke's number.

All fourteen messages had been from Yorke.

All about the same thing.

His family.

Something had happened to his family.

He hit the call button and retched again. He spat bile on the trunk. As the phone rang, he replayed the most reassuring of Yorke's words in his head over and over. *"Frank is fine, Jake. You have my word. Stay calm. He's fine."* But no mention of Sheila—no mention of the woman he once loved more than air itself: *his son's mother.*

"DCI Michael Yorke—"

"Mike, Jesus, thank God, Mike. It's me!"

"Jake ... It's bloody good to hear your voice. I didn't know—"

"What's happened? My family!"

"Be calm, Jake. I need you to be calm."

"Frank? Where's Frank?"

"He's safe. He's with his grandmother."

Thank God, thank God .... Yorke had been telling him the truth. He steadied himself against the tree. He took a deep breath. "Mike ..." He didn't want to ask. He desperately didn't want to know, but ... "Sheila?"

A pause. As good as a confirmation.

Jake punched the tree.

"I'm sorry, Jake ..."

"Fuck! Fuck!"

"I really am."

"Did *they* do it?"

"There's no evidence—"

"Bullshit! Did they do it?"

"I don't know, Jake. Genuinely. It was a gas explosion. Sheila was there. Your son was with her mother, fortunately, so—"

"Jesus! They meant to kill *both* of them? Barbarians."

He punched the tree again. He felt the bark bite deep into his knuckles. *"Fucking barbarians."*

"I'm sorry, Jake. I wish I knew more. The fire service has it down to a faulty gas pipe. There is nothing else there—"

"There doesn't need to be anything else, Mike! You know that. *You* know what we're dealing with. My son. Jesus Christ! My son." He looked at his bleeding knuckles. "What the hell am I going to do?"

"I've been working a rotation. Someone's always watching Frank at his grandmother's. No one will get to him. It has been buying me time to find out more."

"You won't find out anything." *Because Superintendent Joan Madden won't let you.*

He held back on this last bit, because Yorke didn't know that Superintendent Joan Madden was in the pockets of Article SE. He'd assumed that having that information was the only thing keeping his family alive. It seemed Article SE no longer cared about what he knew. Still, he refrained from telling Yorke because it may prove important in the days ahead.

"I'll keep trying, Jake. You have my word. I won't stop."

"It's not enough, Mike. Article SE are the sneakiest group of bastards there is. I need you to get Frank yourself. I need you to get him to safety."

Yorke didn't respond.

"Mike?"

"Jake ... come on ... How can I do that?"

"Easy, you—"

"No, Jake, it isn't easy. His grandmother has temporary custody. It's not as easy as marching in there and taking him."

"Explain the situation to her."

"Would she listen?"

Jake recalled the stubborn nature of his mother-in-law. "Not to me, she wouldn't. But you're different, Mike. She may listen to someone who's, you know ..." *Less of a goddamned fuck up.*

"Taking that child is not a situation I can orchestrate, Jake. Not without causing a lot of problems. We don't even know, for sure, that the problem exists. Gas explosions do happen. They're rare, but they *do* happen."

"She was murdered. And if I don't come home, they'll kill my son too."

"Let's be positive. The round-the-clock protection won't stop."

"Until someone above you puts a stop to it." *Superintendent Joan Madden for example?*

"Over my dead body, Jake."

"I'm coming home."

"You know I want you to come back. You know that's what I've always wanted, but it was always going to be below the radar. Coming back in this state, with this emotion, surely it's a recipe for disaster. Let me keep looking into—"

"I'm coming back, Mike. I'm coming back for my boy."

"Jake—"

"Don't take your eyes off him. I beg of you. With every part of my soul, I beg of you. Do not take your eyes off Frank." Jake hung up and pocketed the cellphone. He wiped the back of his bloody hand on his shirt and winced over the stinging sensation. He glared at the forested hill that led to the Nucleus.

This isn't your world.

This isn't your problem.

He took a deep breath, pictured his young boy dealing with the loss of his mother, and turned back for the town.

Several steps later, he lowered into a crouch. He felt as if he'd been punched in the stomach.

Celestia.

He recalled that first day he had met her on the bench—two lost souls coming together. The pain in their conversation ...

"The sadness, Frank. Around your eyes. There's a lot of it."

"I could say the same of you, Celestia."

"And you'd be right."

"What does a seventeen-year-old girl have to be sad about anyway?"

"What does a thirtysomething man thousands of miles from home have to be sad about?"

"It's that stalemate again, isn't it?"

He recalled their walk to the old mine, his prying questions and his desperation to know who she truly was ...

"Celestia, we have to talk."

"That's what I thought we were doing!"

"No. Talk ... seriously."

"Serious, as in ranking Martin Scorsese films?"

Jake pointed at the hill in the other direction. "Do you have a cinema up there?"

"If you know about that, why are you standing here?"

"Why wouldn't I be?"

"When people around here know you're from the Nucleus, they never give you any trouble, which I guess is a good thing, but neither do they want to talk to you."

"I'm not from around here, and I'd like to know about your home."

"Can we just go back to ranking Scorsese films?"

With tears streaking his face, he recalled the burning of the Dwelling and the rats again and the aftermath

when Celestia had admitted to finally understanding him
...

"I don't know who you think I am, Celestia, but that really isn't me."

"I think it is you."

"You don't know *me. You don't know the real me."*

"I know you care. You care about others more than yourself. I know you need *to help. What would happen if you just stopped?"*

"I wish I knew. I've been trying for God knows how long."

"Stay, Jake. Stay, and help us."

"Even if I stayed, I won't be a match for what is coming."

She hugged him. "Whatever you do, I will always love you for everything you did for me. For us."

"I can't stay." Jake hugged her back. "I'm sorry, Celestia."

"Don't be sorry. A man like you doesn't deserve to spend his entire life being sorry."

Jake wiped away his tears and pushed down the memories. He stood and stared ahead where Brady Crossing and his ticket home awaited him. He turned toward the hill and the Nucleus.

And started to run.

* * *

While she waited for her people to gather in the square, Corrie surveyed the bloodstained platform she stood on— her father's blood. *Her* blood.

She knew it was dangerous to consider what could have been, but she considered it, nonetheless. *Could I have developed a relationship with a man who'd been nothing but a stranger to me? Could he have given Marston the guidance I seemed unable to? Would he have fought for me and my people?*

Strange times brought strange feelings. She fought them back. Albert had been a means to an end. A *successful* one. Spilling her own blood on this platform had set the Nucleus on the right path again.

She regarded her small crowd of almost thirty. She counted eleven children; her own son, Marston, was missing. She sighed again. *My lost boy.*

She addressed her people. "Behind me stands Everlyn, leader of your loyal soldiers, people of the Nucleus. Today, we retaliated because of what happened to our beloved soldiers, Thaxton and Walker. Unfortunately, Glynnie was also lost in battle, but she died as all of us should die—bravely and with love in her heart for the Nucleus."

The cheers seemed subdued, but then the crowd *was* small, so she put it down to paranoia. She did notice Leander, the elderly man who had been particularly vocal during her ascension, clapping with some verve. She smiled over this, then turned to nod her gratitude at each of the three soldiers in turn.

Once the cheering had stopped, several young children near the front of the crowd continued whooping, clearly enjoying festive feel. The fathers of both children stepped forward and placed their hands on the children's shoulders to signal for them to stop.

"Let them," Corrie said. "Let them rejoice. We've won this battle, and now—"

"Won?" Olin asked, leader of the charge, the hunters who shouldered the responsibility of feeding the Nucleus. "How can you suggest that we have won?"

Corrie was surprised; maybe she wasn't being paranoid

after all? "Oh, yes, Olin, *we've* won. We fought them back in the forest, and we marched on them in Brady Crossing. They cowered in their stores as we smashed them to pieces. The only person who had any fight in them is no more. I also met their law enforcement—what was left of it. And you know what the law did? *Begged* me for peace."

Some of the adults in the crowd laughed.

"The sheriff always was weak," Nella called out.

"The sheriff is being shut down as we speak. The law *has* no leadership. Brady Crossing *has* no leadership. You have leadership. What do we have to fear?"

The crowd cheered again.

"Today, while our loyal soldiers redistribute the traps around our lands and restore our defenses, you shall celebrate. Here in the square." Corrie extended a hand as Fern and Ibre carried in two wooden barrels full of beer. "Beer and wine."

* * *

From the distance came the sound of clapping and cheering.

Celestia felt the deep bite of anxiety. Was Corrie back and playing to the crowd again? She recalled Albert's execution with a shudder. What was the tyrant offering now? A victory party to celebrate surviving the assault on Brady Crossing? It made sense to sell the vandalism of Main Street as a clear indication of Mossbark's weakness, but did Corrie really believe this was a war she could win?

Since Celestia had found Logan crammed into the cage, he'd been mumbling, desperately trying to tell her something, so she reached through the bars for the tape around his mouth.

Logan leaned forward as much as he could with such limited space, groaning.

"Just a bit farther ..." she said. "Just a little bit more ..." She managed to grip the edge of the tape and tear it loose.

He winced. "Marston! It's Marston! Look at my head ... He hit me outside my rig and ..."

She felt tightness gripping her chest as Logan's watering eyes darted up, sighting something.

"Behind you!"

Shit ... She bolted up and grabbed the shotgun in one hand from the top of the cage.

"He's got a knife!"

She turned quickly, unable to wield the shotgun with any skill.

Marston had come close against her so the shotgun shaft rested uselessly against his left arm.

She looked into his tiny eyes. They were cold and unmoving. "Marston—" The wind was forced out of her. She felt a sudden chill in her stomach and saw his right hand clasped around the hilt of the knife. "No, Marston—"

He pulled the blade free, and she collapsed to the floor.

18

Lyman loved peace and quiet. It was the reason he loved his sentry job. Bar a recent explosion on Netow's bend and an occasional drunken trespasser drawn to the mystery in their hills, drama was at a premium at the Nucleus's entrance. So, between requests from Nucleus residents requesting access through the raising arm barrier, Lyman managed to do a fair bit of reading.

Not literature. Not books of any kind. Not even nonfiction or newspapers. Only magazines. Sports, men's health, travel—he'd even been known to delve into a fashion magazine or two.

His wife, Rena, claimed it was just the glossy, computer-enhanced images that had him hooked; he argued that it was down to his innate curiosity and thirst for knowledge.

The reason wasn't important to him. What was important to him was he had piles of them in the corners of the sentry hut and had lots to get through before next month's run into town. Hence his irritation when he heard the rumble of an approaching engine. He'd just reached a rather engaging bit in a food magazine about the best way to spit roast, and the hog didn't half look sumptuous.

"Shit!" He threw down the magazine and stepped from the hut with his binoculars.

Admittedly, he did feel some curiosity, because he'd already welcomed Corrie and her party back earlier, but it was nothing compared to the intense curiosity he felt over how to get a spit-roasted hog to look as good as it did on the—

He looked through the binoculars, and his heart thudded in his chest. Curiosity had just gone off the scale. An unrecognizable pickup was quickly approaching up the hill. He dove back into the sentry hut for his walkie-talkie. "Lyman calling Everlyn?"

"Go ahead."

"We've an unidentified vehicle heading up to the barrier. Over."

"Copy. We were en route to the southernmost forest to rearm. We will change direction. Pin them down until we get there. Over."

Lyman threw down the walkie-talkie and swooped for his rifle.

The pickup crested the top of the hill, showing no signs of slowing.

"Shit!" Lyman pinned the rifle sight to his eyes. *I'm in unprecedented waters here.* He aimed for the windshield and took a shot. He missed. "Shit!" *Too much time reading and not enough time practicing your shooting, Lyman.*

The pickup came up a dirt road with some speed now, generating a swirling dust cloud. It looked as if the wind were propelling it.

Lyman, feeling his lunch turning around in his stomach,

steadied the rifle with sweating hands. He fired. He missed. "Shit!"

The pickup was only fifty or so yards away now; he really didn't have too many more chances at this. Ignoring the gurgle in his stomach, he aimed and fired.

The pickup's windshield exploded.

"Yes!" Lyman whooped. "Yes, you fucker."

The pickup continued at an unrelenting pace.

Fuck ... Fuck ... the driver is still in control. He aimed and fired again.

The pickup continued.

Lyman could see the driver now, hunched over his wheel, propelling it onward. Lyman gulped and with trembling hands, took a final shot. He didn't know if he'd hit the driver, because the vehicle knocked the wind out of him and drove him backward into his sentry hut.

He felt the wood crashing down around him, and he died on a pile of his beloved magazines.

After Everlyn, Ibre, and Fern had taken leave to rearm the southernmost forest, Corrie paced alone behind the platform, ignoring the celebrations and feeling far less content than she should have been, considering.

But it came down to this. How could she relish the emancipation of the Nucleus from the vile descendants of Althea without her boy by her side? As much as she tried to tell herself that the Nucleus was everything, it wasn't. Marston factored above all.

So she'd ventured back to the Focus, to *Marston*, by taking a more obscure back route that looped nearer to the entrance of the Nucleus, rather than the southernmost forest, to avoid being sighted by Everlyn and the soldiers. She didn't want to air her vulnerability over Marston. She needed them to believe she remained completely focused on the strengthening of the Nucleus in its new form. That way they would continue to follow her—into the fire, if necessary; exactly how they had done earlier in Brady Crossing.

Having circled around, she entered the Focus at the rear. Knowing everyone was celebrating in the square, she wasn't cautious and strolled down the central walkway, lost to thoughts of tactics and strategy—

She heard knocking ahead and halted. She had drawn level with the cabin adjacent to hers and was certain that whoever was knocking was doing so on *her* door. The entrance to the cabins of the Focus faced west, the direction Corrie was walking from, so whoever was at her door could not yet see her.

She heard another knock, followed by a loud familiar voice. "If no one is going to answer, I'm coming in."

She took a deep breath. *What the hell was Frank doing back here? And at her door?* She changed direction and darted in so she was pinned against the side of the adjacent cabin. Then she slid free a holstered gun from beneath her unbuttoned cotton shirt. She worked her way along the side of the cabin and peered around at her entrance at the exact moment Frank came good on his promise of entering.

He wasn't holding her firearm, but, of course, that didn't mean he wasn't packing. She kept a tight, two-handed grip on her weapon and edged herself into the open *after* he'd disappeared inside.

"Celestia!" Frank exclaimed.

Celestia? She came for me! Corrie thought. *The bitch only went and came back for me!* As Corrie closed the gap to the entrance to her cabin, she could hear voices but was unsure as to what they were saying. She moved quickly to her front door. There was no time for any caution. Her son was in there. She approached the front door and peered around into the gloom and took a deep breath over what she saw.

A lot of blood.

When she was certain her son was not in there, she pulled her head back, pinned herself beside the door, and listened to the conversation inside.

Everlyn held her hand in the air. "Careful."

The crunching of boots in the undergrowth halted.

She pinned binoculars to her eyes and traced a plume of smoke to the pickup Lyman had warned them about. She studied its position, determining it had plowed through the sentry hut and collided with a tree. Someone was hunched over the wheel.

"Have you tried Lyman again?" Everlyn asked.

"Still no answer," Ibre said.

"Ditch the walkie-talkie. Lyman's gone."

"How do you know?"

"The sentry hut. Look." She held the binoculars over her shoulder so Ibre could look.

"Shit ... you think the driver came alone?" Ibre asked. "He looks like he did a right number on himself."

"We assume there're more." Everlyn turned. "Listen up. I'll go down the middle. Ibre, you circle around to the side of the pickup this way." She pointed southward. "And, Fern, the other way ... If anyone else was in that vehicle, we'll squeeze them out." Everlyn didn't wait for a response.

They were short on time. They couldn't risk *anyone* breaching their last line of defense.

The crash had happened moments ago. She still had the opportunity to put this right.

As she weaved down the dirt path toward the scene of the accident, she listened to the footfalls of her comrades as they fanned out. Eventually, the footsteps quietened, then stopped.

They were good, her fighters. Ever so good. She didn't tell them often enough. She would most certainly tell them later. She would also allow them some time to grieve for Glynnie. Losing Glynnie had been a major blow. She'd been a loyal friend and a loyal fighter, and neither of them had been allowed a moment to reflect yet.

One last push, soldiers. One last push and we will shore up these defenses tighter than they've ever been ... and we'll take that well-earned respite.

She paused at the parking lot en route to the entrance and waved her rifle over the seven vehicles. She squinted, trying to detect movement of any kind, but sensed nothing. Maybe she should check them more thoroughly? She looked forward where the wreckage was and remained confident that any intruders, if there had been any more of them, wouldn't have made it this far in.

She continued, fully aware that she, out of the three of them, trod the most dangerous path. Out here, on this dirt track, she was a sitting duck to anyone hiding in the surrounding trees. Her companions could move more stealthily in their approach through the woodland, taking cover, and using their knowledge of their landscape to gain advantage over intruders. However, she remained their leader, and she'd never shied from leading by example. Plus, she'd sent one of her soldiers to their death today already; she certainly couldn't cope with doing that again.

She'd always been good under pressure, but as she reached the end of the dirt path, she made several erratic 360-degree spins while jabbing her rifle in the air. *Come on, fuckers. If you're here, show yourself!*

When it was clear that she'd just succumbed to a wave of anxiety, she took a deep breath and stilled herself. *Calm yourself, Everlyn. Calm yourself.* It had been a trying day, but control in an occupation such as this one was an absolutely must.

When she reached the front of the smoking pickup, she kept the rifle trained on the driver hunched over the wheel. He was still, and she was almost certain he was dead, but she'd never been in the business of taking unnecessary risks. When she was close enough, she prodded the driver through the smashed windshield, causing him to slump back and away from the wheel. His chest was drenched in blood, and his eyes were wide.

At least you got the fucker, Lyman.

Speaking of Lyman ... She took several steps alongside the pickup and saw the wreckage of the sentry hut just behind it. Lyman's twisted legs poked out from beneath several layers of wood. His shoulders and head were also exposed and rested upon a scattered pile of bloody magazines. His teeth were clenched, and his lips were drawn back—

Footsteps.

She raised her eyes and her weapon and saw Fern stalking toward her. She still had both hands on the rifle and flitted her eyes cautiously from side to side.

When Fern reached Everlyn, she shook her head and

mouthed, *Nothing.* She gestured behind Everlyn with a nod.

Everlyn turned to see Ibre approaching from the other side of the pickup, also empty handed. He shrugged.

Everlyn nodded to show she understood, but she still didn't feel secure. Not yet. She turned in a circle, surveying the area. She looked at Ibre again. "Stay vigilant—"

A crack of a rifle erupted, and Ibre's kneecap exploded. He toppled sideways, thudding to the ground. While Ibre howled, Everlyn turned again, desperately searching for the source of the gunshot. "Fern... dammit ... Can you see—"

Another gunshot. The howling stopped. Ibre's skull had been reduced to blood and bone.

"Get away from the pickup!" Everlyn darted backward. "Someone's under the pick—" She went over Lyman's legs. On the ground, she looked deep into the eyes of the man beneath the pickup and desperately tried to turn the rifle in his direction, but she saw the muzzle of his rifle flash, and it felt like someone had punched her in the throat. Gasping and gurgling, she turned her gaze to Fern, who was running.

Stand and fight, soldier!

Choking on blood, Everlyn watched a man roll clear of a large piece of wood that had once formed a wall of the sentry hut and was now propped against a tree. Everlyn watched Fern take a bullet in her back as it dawned on her that her throat was ruined, and that she'd already taken her last breath.

19

Gordon stared at the walkie-talkie in his hand when it crackled into life.

Nicholas Brannagh's voice broke free. "It's done. We lost Ronald, but we got three of the bastards who came down to Brady. I repeat: three of the bastards *are* down. Over."

"And the fourth?" Gordon asked. "Where is the fourth?"

"We saw only three. Over."

Gordon eyed Scott standing beside him. The spineless little fuck was as pale as ice. Gordon smiled at him. *You will burn here with the rest of them, traitor.*

He turned to look at the nine armed men who'd followed him through the southernmost forest right up to the rotten core. Their expressions were serious. He tuned back and spoke into the walkie-talkie. "Well done, Nicholas. You've weakened them. And now we can put an end to this —especially as Mossbark's most popular butcher, you selected very capable citizens. Over."

182

"Guess I'm in the right job to do so. Not many vegetarians in Mossbark after all. Over."

"Well, after we clear this land, you'll have more land to hunt on. You'll have to increase storage." Gordon laughed. "Over."

"Guess so. Hadn't thought about it. Over."

But you have, haven't you? Gordon thought with a sneer. *Why else would you be here otherwise? And I'm sure all these loyal men following me to the center of the Nucleus have their eye on something too ...* "We'll see you in that square at the center, Nicholas. Over."

"Are you sure the rest of the people are there? Over."

"They're there. I can hear them whooping, hollering, playing their goddamned guitars—having the time of their fucking lives, after everything they've done to us over the years. *Everything.* Over and out."

Everything I let happen. Just like I let you fuck me, Susan. Walk over me like a dirty rug. Well, you're done, and this place is done too.

Scott came up close to him as they marched past the residential area. "Surely that's enough now, Sheriff. Without their soldiers, they'll wither."

"We have scorched the snake, son, but we haven't killed it."

"But does there need to be any more bloodshed, boss?"

Gordon turned to Scott. "What do you think I am? A monster? They'll get a choice."

"A choice?"

"To leave, or ..." He gestured at the men trudging in a line and raised his eyebrows. "They wouldn't be stupid enough to opt for the alternative, would they?"

"They're proud people. I can't be part of this, Sheriff."

Gordon put his hands on Scott's shoulders. "I've arrived

here to get my dignity back, son. I'm not leaving without it."
*And for that to happen, you won't be able to leave either, son.
At least not in one piece.*

* * *

Clutching her stomach, Celestia sat against the wall
between both bedroom doors. Her shirt was drenched in
blood.

"Celestia!" Jake sprang forward and almost slipped over
the blood trail. He steadied himself against the wall and
knelt beside her.

She looked up at him with weary eyes and managed a
smile. "Jake ... Marston took me by surprise."

"Where is he?"

"Gone. He stabbed me and ran."

"Frank ... Jake, even! In here!"

"*Logan!* Are you okay?"

"Yes ... but I need your help, pronto."

Jake shook his head as he looked at Celestia's pale face.
"She needs to get out of here *right now*."

"Precisely why your ass is required in here *now*."

Jake rose and looked around the bedroom door. "A
cage? Shit."

"Little bastard clocked me outside my rig, and I woke up
here. There's a reason fourteen-year-olds shouldn't be
allowed to drive."

"Celestia, keep pressing that wound."

"Yes, boss." She groaned.

"What the hell did Marston want from you anyway?"
Jake went into the bedroom.

"His psycho mother sent him. They wanted to drive you
out of the Nucleus on a mission to find me so they could

take a free run at Celestia. Seems I was deemed surplus to requirements when they brought Albert here, because his death sent you packing anyway."

Jake knelt to examine the padlock. "I'll need to find something to break through this."

"That'll do." Logan nodded to the side.

Jake followed his gaze to the edge of the room and saw the shotgun he'd furnished Celestia with at Albert's store. He stood and went over to grab it. He cracked it and saw, with no small measure of relief, it was still loaded. "Celestia ..."

"Yes?"

"Loud noise coming but keep your hands on the wound."

"Okay."

"Now get yourself as far back as you can, Logan."

"Are you joking, man?" Logan said. "On account of being fat, I've used up every spare inch."

"Guess I can't expect you to cover your ears, then?"

"You notice my hands tied behind my back, or do you think I'm Houdini?"

Jake pointed the shotgun down and blew off the padlock.

"Jesus, how about a countdown at least?"

Jake placed the smoking shotgun on top of the cage and stepped backward to allow Logan to slip clear. He knelt to untie the rope that bound his wrists behind his back.

Logan winced and groaned as he stretched his hands in front of him, then rose slowly to his feet, grunting. "I feel like I've been folded up and posted in an envelope."

"We need to go." Jake stepped from the room.

Logan followed.

Jake spied his friend, and his heart sank again. "We need to get you help now, Celestia."

Celestia nodded. "Don't worry. Remember *Reservoir Dogs*?" She paused to catch her breath. "Mr. Orange lasted a long time with that gut wound."

"Actually, that was a bullet," Logan said, "Not a blade—"

Jake glared at him.

Logan scrunched his face. "Yeah ... sorry ... bad time to correct."

"Listen, Celestia," Jake said. "You're going to put an arm around me and one around Logan. Then—"

The room darkened. As the curtains were drawn, most of the light had been coming through the open front door.

Jake flitted his eyes right to see Corrie blocking the sun. He faced her, opening his mouth to speak, but a loud bang sounded, and the air was taken from his body before any words could emerge. He went to his knees, sucking back air, and clutched his gut.

Corrie entered the room. "Talk about having everything tied up in a neat little bow."

Jake looked down and saw blood spilling out the cracks between his fingers. He looked up to see her pointing the gun at Logan.

"I mean, you'll just be collateral damage, but you ..." She pointed the gun at Jake. "And you"—she moved it to Celestia—"well ... let's just say I struck gold."

Corrie stepped forward, smirking. "Did you come to kill me, Celestia?"

"You deserve it," Celestia hissed.

"Maybe. But it seems your family has a habit of failing. First, your father. And now, you." She kept the gun moving between the targets as she drew closer to Jake. She paused and scrunched her face. "You just don't get it, do you, Celestia? I've buried my husband, my daughter, and today, my father. All because of you. *Your family.* I've lost everyone apart from Marston. If that doesn't make a person resilient and determined, what will?" She pointed the gun down at Jake's head. "So, enjoy this, Celestia. Enjoy watching your boyfriend die—"

Anticipating what was coming and getting final confirmation with that last word, Jake swooped as she fired. He screamed in agony as the bullet tore into his left shoulder. He threw out his right hand, grabbed her wrist, and dragged her close—

Her fist pounded into his face, but he refused to let it cut off his adrenaline, and even when she started to scratch him, the pain was incomparable to what was already raging through his body from the shoulder and stomach wounds.

He dragged her down so hard that he felt her wrist snap in his hand. With her grip now ruined, the gun clattered to the ground. From the corner of his eyes, Jake saw Logan swoop for the weapon. Jake grabbed Corrie's throat.

"Okay, I've got the gun!" Logan said.

Despite feeling like every pain receptor was on fire, Jake yanked himself up Corrie's body and glared into her wide eyes. He tightened his grip further.

"Frank ... Jake ... I've got you covered!" Logan continued.

Corrie's eyes bulged.

Jake squeezed harder.

"Let go, Jake!"

Corrie was changing color.

Jake gritted his teeth.

Logan's hands were on his back, pulling at him, but he shrugged them off.

"Jake, please!"

Corrie's tongue was poking out from between her lips.

He *then* saw Sheila banging on the window of their home as the fire tore into the room behind her; Celestia gripping her stomach, trying to hold in her damaged organs; Peter, his eyes rolled back, pointing toward the bullet hole in his head; Lillian broken at the bottom of the cliff; and Paul Conway, the dead boy in his arms, ruined by a car bomb.

And he squeezed and squeezed *and* squeezed.

Afterward, he slumped onto the floor, clutching his stomach and studying Corrie's pale, dead face. He regarded Logan. "Gut wound *from a* bullet ... *Reservoir Dogs.* Happy now?"

Logan sighed and shook his head. "I'm not happy, Jake. And forget the gut; your shoulder looks worse."

* * *

Gordon and Scott passed a long rectangular wooden structure and entered the square. After many weeks of drone surveillance, Gordon knew the layout of the Nucleus like the back of his hand, and he strode with confidence.

Admittedly, the nine willing fighters unearthed by Nicholas Brannagh, who stalked behind him, formed no small part of that confidence.

In the center, several couples danced enthusiastically to the sound of acoustic guitars. A small cluster of people glugged back ale around some barrels alongside a raised platform. Children chased each other around the perimeter, giggling wildly.

"There're so many children," Scott said.

Gordon shrugged. "And about twenty or so adults."

"But children! We can't do this, Sheriff. We can't."

Gordon glared at him. "Man up, son. You're a sheriff deputy. The people before you have been breaking the law for time immemorial. You are here to uphold it."

"I joined the sheriff's department to keep the peace."

"Well, in order for us to have peace, we first have to stop the goddamned lawbreaking."

"They're having a party, Sheriff. They're not waving machetes!"

"A party." Again, he surveyed the cavorting couples—the two elderly men on stools, hammering their acoustic guitars for everything they were worth, and the people swilling beverages by the platform. "A party on land that don't belong to them." He put his hand in the air to signal the men behind him. "On land that *never* belonged to them."

The men stepped forward and fanned out around Gordon and Scott.

One of the younger men, gifted with some dexterity and energy in his dance moves so it was verging on jive, noticed first. He jabbed a finger in their direction and shouted, "Intruders!"

The guitars stopped, and the dancers, as well as the group of six or so people around the beers, turned and stared, wide-eyed, as Gordon's men formed a semi-circle around the square.

Bizarrely, despite the sudden standoff, the playful shouts of the youngsters continued as they raucously chased one another.

Gordon shot his gun in the air and silenced everyone. "Now, listen—"

The dancing couples and those supping over at the barrels shouted for their children. The children, programmed to respond to their parents' signals, reacted instantly, screaming as they sprinted into the square and into their parents' arms.

Gordon kept his eyes peeled for weapons in the panicked scene. He waited until the families were reunited before firing a second bullet into the air, silencing the crowd once again. "It's over!" Gordon panned left and right to check that the men, who'd fanned into that semi-circle, were ready on their rifles so he wasn't making himself an easy target, then stepped forward. "I'm Sheriff Gordon Kane."

"We know who you are," one of the guitar-playing old men said.

"Good. Then you know how serious this is."

"Until recently, I don't remember the Sheriff of Moss-bark taking one goddamned thing seriously."

"Who're you?"

"Leander."

"Well, Leander, if you knew who I was—I mean, *really* knew who I was—you'd know I'm here to reclaim land that belongs to us."

"Are you serious?"

"Over this matter, I am *deadly* fucking serious."

"This land belongs to us!"

"Not true. It was ours long before you infected it."

"Nobody wanted these lands!" Leander put his guitar on the ground. "You lot wanted the coal. We respected that and let you keep your mines. Your industry dies, so now you look over your shoulders at what we have?" He rose from his stool. "Have you seen your fucking town, Sheriff? It sparkles. And who was it that made it sparkle?"

"You did. But at a cost. Our complicity. You hollowed out *many* other towns to feed yourselves."

"And to keep you well fed too, don't you forget that."

"You're parasites. It's not who *we* are."

"Yet, you're the one standing here with guns. How many? Nine or ten of you? Pointing guns at children. *Children!*"

"Holier than thou, Leander, are you? Your people came to our town tonight, killed an innocent man. Blew him to fucking pieces in his own store."

"And you came to us *earlier*, killing Thaxton and Walker." He pointed at a middle-aged woman standing by the barrel of beer. "Cathenne, Thaxton's wife. Maybe you should ask her how she feels about that?"

He didn't need to. The expression of disgust said it all.

"This is over," Gordon said. "I made mistakes, but we all make mistakes. The person who realizes their mistakes, then puts them right, atones."

"Pointing rifles at going on ten children is probably the most fucked-up atonement I've ever come across!"

"Come on, Leander!" Gordon guffawed. "We *all* know the stories. How your own soldiers rounded up the children under Griffin and awaited orders to execute them!"

"You won't find a single person here that condoned what happened that day."

"Bullshit," Gordon said. "You're fucking puppets, and you'll follow whoever speaks the loudest, like wild animals succumbing to a goddamned alpha. This ends now. My atonement comes from giving Mossbark their freedom back. It will be its own county again and not some cowering shit show, beholden to their wild animals and whatever alpha is in charge."

"And then what happens to you, Sheriff? You've placed yourself above whatever laws you hold valuable. You think they'll just let you be?"

"No, I don't. But, you see, I've accepted my fate. I'm at

peace with it. You speak boldly for your people, but it's in vain. You're reasoning with a man who has nothing left to lose."

"Sounds like bullshit to me." Leander looked over his shoulder toward the raised platform.

Gordon knew exactly what he was looking for. "Your soldiers?"

Leander turned back and narrowed his eyes.

"The soldiers who came to Brady Crossing so full of confidence?" Gordon said. "The ones who believed us weak?"

Leander paled.

"Their error. And we've not made the same one. We showed your soldiers the respect they didn't show us. We appreciated their skillset." Gordon smiled. "Which is why we eliminated them before coming to you."

Leander opened his mouth to speak, but nothing came out. He scanned the line of men who had every inch of the square covered with rifles.

"Now that you know it's over, listen carefully. It's time for you all to leave. If you do this without any trouble, then you've my word that no one else will be hurt."

"What do you expect us to do? Where do you expect us to go?" a woman called out from close to the barrels. She stood close to Cathanne, wife of the late Thaxton, who was still staring at Gordon with fury.

"And you are?" Gordon said.

"Nella."

"Well, Nella. Frankly, I don't care. The southernmost forest is disarmed. You'll walk through that forest, and you'll walk away from Mossbark County. Your reward for doing that is your lives. If you ever choose to return, you'll forfeit them."

"But *our* homes," Nella said. "Our homes are here."

"We'll burn your homes to the ground. We'll eradicate every trace of you ever being here. This isn't the world of the Nucleus any longer. It never really was."

"Will you not even allow us into our homes to get supplies? Clothing?" Nella asked.

"Surely, that makes sense?" Scott said.

Gordon glared at him and hissed, "And then they arm themselves! Our situation is perfect. We have complete control, and you want to show them mercy after what they've caused? What they started?"

"I just think—"

"She's armed!" one of the armed men shouted.

"Cathanne, don't!" Leander called.

Gordon did not have his own weapon readied, so he watched, open mouthed, as Thaxton's widow raised a rifle.

"You murderer!" she screamed and fired.

Gordon expected to be hit, so when he stumbled sideways, he assumed it was the force of a bullet.

It wasn't.

He'd just lost his footing during the surprise. He'd gotten lucky.

"No!" Nella said, realizing the danger, and pushed down Cathanne's rifle.

But the armed men behind Gordon were drunk on adrenaline, and they'd seen enough.

They open fired.

* * *

When Jake heard continuous gunfire, he clenched Celestia's hand and looked into her eyes. It was loud, and it was close. It was a clear indication that the time of the Nucleus was coming to an end.

Both Jake and Celestia were sitting against the wall of the cabin, bleeding, while Logan paced in front of them, muttering, "We have to go. We have to go now."

Wincing over the pain consuming his body, Jake eyed his friend. "Logan, my front pocket."

Logan nodded, knelt, and retrieved Jake's cellphone.

"I need you to do something. It's the most important thing I've ever asked anyone to do."

"I understand, partner."

"My code ... Twenty-five, five. Twenty-five, five ... My son's birthday. Say it back."

"Twenty-five, five."

"*Again.*"

"Twenty-five, five."

"If, for whatever reason, I don't make it, I want you to call Mike Yorke. He's a cop in the UK ... you can just hit redial."

"Okay. And?"

"And ..." He glanced at Celestia, trying to hide his guilty look. "And tell him that I'm done. *Finished.* Tell him what happened here so the bastards who want me back home can get the news they've been desperate to hear."

Celestia gripped his hand tighter. "No—"

"Celestia ... listen ... this is the best thing. I can finally free my son from danger. It's all I've ever wanted." He refocused on Logan. "Now help her up."

Logan came forward, knelt, helped Celestia get her arm around his shoulder, and helped her to her feet. She moaned as she rose, but once on her feet, Jake saw, with some relief, she could walk, with Logan taking most of her weight.

"Okay ..." Jake stared up at Logan. "*Go.*"

Celestia's eyes widened "I'm not leaving you ... You need help too—"

"*Go, now.*" Jake looked at Celestia. "They'll be here soon. And I'll follow. I promise I'll give it everything I've got."

Celestia shook her head. "No ... We can go together. Logan can help us both."

Jake watched Logan lower his head, clearly as distressed by this situation as Celestia but far more accepting of the reality.

"You give him too much credit," Jake said with a smile. "He isn't that strong."

Logan smiled but didn't raise his eyes to look at Jake again, probably fearful he might tear up.

"This isn't your war, Jake," Celestia said. "This isn't your fight—"

"But it's my *decision*. Now get out of here. Please. Before I lose two more of my closest friends. I got this. I've been in worst situations."

Logan nodded. "He's right. We're going now, Celestia." He started to turn from Jake, guiding Celestia with him.

"No," Celestia said. "We can't. We *just* can't."

Outside, the gunfire had ceased. It wouldn't be long until the intruders descended into the Focus.

"I will follow. *With everything I have,*" Jake said.

Supporting Celestia, Logan approached the exit.

Logan glanced back. "Good luck, partner."

"You too, buddy. Remember, twenty-five, five ...."

Logan nodded. "Twenty-five, five."

Just before the exit, Celestia looked back at Jake, her eyes full of tears. "I love you, Jake."

"I love you too, Celestia, and I'll see you soon. Bank on it."

After they disappeared through the door, Jake gritted his teeth, took a deep breath, and attempted to get to his feet. The pain, combined with the loss of blood, had him beaten though, and he only managed to slide himself halfway up the wall, before sliding back down again.

He sighed and thought of Frank.

He thought of his son's freedom now that Jake served no purpose to Article SE.

He closed his eyes and smiled.

* * *

Not a single shot had been returned.

When Gordon saw a woman clutching her broken child to her bosom, he opened his mouth to call for a ceasefire—

"Stop!" Scott shouted. "In the name of God, *stop*!"

The trigger-happy residents of Mossbark continued to spray the area. Those in the firing line who hadn't yet fallen took cover behind the platform and beer barrels.

"They're not even armed!" Scott continued. "You're shooting *children*!"

This seemed to have an effect. Some of the men stopped firing.

Gordon added to Scott's calls. "Enough!"

The gunfire stopped.

Gordon surveyed. Bodies lay twisted and bloodied. The old man, Leander, was bent over his smashed acoustic guitar with an outstretched palm in the air, his only defense against the bullets that'd killed him. The area by the barrels had been the worst hit, as this was where Cathanne had raised her rifle. About eight people were folded over each other here, forming an image of death that was destined to forever plague these men's dreams.

The butcher, Nicholas Brannagh, and one other man emerged from the trees behind the platform. The two men raised their weapons and pointed them at the surviving residents taking cover there. The children cried, while the parents who had somehow got them to safety, pleaded for mercy.

"No more!" Gordon put a hand in the air, gesturing at Nicholas. He stepped forward and raised his voice so the butcher could hear. "Let them leave Mossbark and never return."

The two men waved the survivors to their feet; the children continued to cry, while the adults, pale and trembling, continued to plead.

"Go *now!*" Gordon shouted.

Rather than opt to run through the square, over the bodies of their loved ones, past the men who had come to wipe out the Nucleus, and down toward the southernmost forest, they headed in the other direction toward the main entrance.

Gordon felt Scott's eyes boring into him. He turned and glared at his traitorous companion. Then he acknowledged the men from Mossbark. "To the residential area to finish this place!"

* * *

Having identified it through his drone surveillance, Gordon could direct the men to the supply of gas that the Nucleus had been using to fuel their vehicles.

Gordon and Scott hung back as, one by one, the men entered the wooden storage facility and emerged with five-gallon metal jerry cans, before proceeding into the residential area of the Nucleus.

"Is this necessary?" Scott asked. "They've left. Those who you spared, ran."

"I spared?" Gordon turned his gaze on Scott. "This is all their doing. Do not make me out to be the cause of their deaths."

"I just watched children die; that's on you, Sheriff."

"I see ..." Gordon nodded. "Is this about your brother?"

"No. Not now, it isn't."

"You, your brother, and Riley followed me into these woods. You knew the risks. All of you did."

"We'd have followed you anywhere, but my brother needed that hospital. We owed it to him."

"You're a big boy now, Scott. You could have taken him yourself when I left you at the station. Why didn't you?"

Scott opened his mouth to reply, but Gordon got there first. "I'll tell you why. Because you knew I was right. You knew that taking him to hospital was a bad idea. You're as much to blame for his death as I am."

Scott flinched. Tears sprang in his eyes. He looked down, shaking his head, summoning the courage to plead one last time. "This has got to end. We're not savages. We shouldn't just burn this place."

"We're doing them a favor, son," Gordon said, watching one of the men kick in a cabin door and enter. "Why leave them with the temptation to return? If their home is no more, they'll stay away, and they'll stay out of danger."

The man emerged from the first cabin and shouted, "Clear!"

At once, another man entered the cabin with a jerry can. Seconds later, he emerged with the can tilted, spilling a line of gasoline several yards from the door. The man surveyed his handiwork, then, with a ghost of a smile on his face, struck a match.

Whoosh.

The first cabin went up in flames, and some of the men cheered.

"Too late." Gordon clapped Scott on the back. "And it's for the best. These bastards are the ones who killed your brother. Enjoy seeing their world turn to ash. You've earned that—"

"I can't believe I thought of you like a father. You're worse than he ever was."

Gordon slapped Scott across the face.

The deputy spat on the ground, turned, and walked away.

* * *

Gordon stood and watched as, one by one, the cabins of the Nucleus ignited in flames. Soon, their world really would be no more. Only seven had survived and were now refugees seeking a haven. They couldn't return to Mossbark County. There was nothing for them here anymore—no friends, no land.

And more importantly, no safety.

Despite thriving under the oppression of the Nucleus, Mossbark County had *still* been oppressed. They'd lived under control and in fear.

No longer.

Gordon had won.

He took a deep breath and listened out for his dead wife. "Not a single word eh, Susan?" he murmured. "Not a word of congratulations? Can you not even find a snide comment in yourself that despite this success, my life is still going to end?" He chuckled to himself as the fiery cabin closest to him collapsed on itself. "My life has been over for a long time, Susan. You made damned sure of that." He pictured his 'I love New York Mug.' "For so long, I have drunk from that mug, trying to find that place ... that time ... when everything was still there."

Ahead, he saw the men clear the final cabin and ready a lighter.

"They'll remember me, Susan. They'll remember me as the person who brought Mossbark County back to its feet—"

The sound of sudden movement beside him made him glance at Scott, followed by a flash of a blade and a cold stinging sensation on his throat. After going to his knees, he watched the final cabin of the Nucleus burst into flames, before falling forward and dying in the dirt.

20

Every morning when Jake opened his eyes, he bolted upright in bed and shouted, *"Frank!* I got you son ... I got you ..." And on every one of those mornings, he felt a hand on his shoulder, pushing him backward onto the bed.

"The stitches ... think of your stitches," the voice of the man who'd come to his aid instructed.

"My son. My son's all that matters," was always Jake's response. Although, he was never quite sure if he'd got the words out or not, because then the pain and the fever would quickly tear him from reality again.

One morning though, he'd enough strength to resist that push back onto the bed, and he knew he was on the mend. He looked his savior in the eyes. "You, of all people."

Scott sat down in the chair beside the bed. "Just because we argued a few times doesn't mean I have it in me to let you bleed out."

Jake recalled the moment he'd managed to get to his feet in the cabin. Pissing blood, he'd staggered free of Corrie's final resting place. Then he'd *heard* them—a crowd of men swarming toward the Focus. He'd moved as fast as his dying legs would allow him, which wasn't fast enough. Still, he had managed to get clear of the cabin before the mob arrived, and even made it to a tree on the edge of the south-ernmost forest, before collapsing. He recalled the fire—*lots* of fire—and then Scott approaching him through the smoke ...

"I remember now." Jake leaned back onto the cushion. "You helped me through that forest."

"I never expected you to make it. You were a mess." He snorted. "I'm sorry to say I kind of hoped you wouldn't. Taking your weight while you hobbled along was no easy task. You also ruined my shirt."

And then it dawned on Jake that despite this man's heroics, he had been there in the Nucleus, and so was one of the posse who had inflicted death and destruction.

"You were one of them ... you were one of the fuckers who burned—"

"No. I was there, I admit, but I didn't pull a single trigger or strike a single match. You may not believe me, but it's the truth. This was all Sheriff Gordon Kane's doing."

"I guess I'll try to believe you ... easier that way ... can't really kill you after you saved my life, can I?" He winced over the persistent pain in his shoulder.

"I'll go and get you some painkillers."

"No ... wait ... There are things I need to know first. What happened to the Nucleus? The people. It can't all be gone?"

Scott looked away. "Yes. All of it. Burned to the ground."

"The people! For pity's sake, where're the children?" Adrenaline surged. He sat upright. His wounded stomach shot him a painful warning.

Scott continued to look away. "I managed to stop them shooting before they were ... you know ... all gone. About seven survived. They ran for their lives. Some of them were children."

"Some! There were nine children in the Nucleus, goddammit!" Jake said, causing himself more pain with the exclamation.

"I'm sorry," Scott said, still looking away. "God forgive me, I know."

"Where've they run to?"

"I don't know. They've left Mossbark County though. They'll be safer."

"Celestia and Logan? Do you know if *they* got away?"

"Logan Reed was there?"

"Yes. Corrie and her son Marston snatched him."

"I didn't see them, sorry."

"How long has it been?"

"Almost a week—"

"A *fucking* week!"

"You were badly injured."

Jake paused to think. *A week.* If Celestia and Logan hadn't been discovered by now, it suggested they'd made it. He felt his spirits lift. "Where's Gordon Kane *now*? Where are those who did this? Who's holding them accountable?"

Scott's eyes widened. "Gordon is dead. He was caught in the crossfire. They found his badly burned body in the wreckage of a smoldering cabin. But, believe me, the shit is hitting the fan for those who took their wrath into those hills. Their plan to keep it from the authorities backfired. Prior to the assault, Gordon murdered a lieutenant from MSP at his home. Not the best move in keeping everything hush-hush. They also discovered his butchered wife there.

The truth is out now, and everyone involved is to be held accountable."

"You were there."

"I was, but I never pulled the trigger or set those fires, as I told you. I was also the one who put the call into MSP, because I knew what the sheriff was capable of." He rubbed his temples. "You know, I begged him not to do what he did ... however, they still suspended me, and I'm under investigation. Maybe those in custody found enough honesty in themselves to back my story, as I still haven't been arrested? I guess only time will tell what my penance will be. But I'm happy to pay it."

"What about me?"

"What about you?"

"Who knows I'm alive?"

"Just me ... oh, and the doctor who treated you."

"The doctor?"

"Yes. You think I could remove the bullets and sew you back up?"

"Where is he?"

"He's gone. We took you off a drip, and I've been feeding you these." He pointed to a packet on the table. "Antibiotics. He wants to remain anonymous. He doesn't want his name involved in this whatsoever. It was damn lucky I had anyone to call. Gordon gave me the number recently; he was originally going to help my brother."

"Your brother?"

Scott lowered his head. "I don't want to go into it now. It's not important to you."

"Could they identify all the bodies at the Nucleus?"

Scott shook his head. "No. Those people never had birth certificates, and they certainly didn't have dental records."

Which meant that if Article SE made inquiries from the UK to find out if Jake was really dead, they could have discovered unidentifiable remains. Would this be enough for them? Well, only time would tell.

"I'll take those painkillers now, please," Jake said.

"Coming right up." Scott stood and stretched. He left the room, and left Jake to his thoughts.

Everyone closest to him would now believe him dead: Mike, Celestia, Logan, and, most painfully, Frank. It was a horrendous feeling, which antagonized him more deeply and more painfully than any gut wound could ever do. Yet, despite the cruel nature of the situation, his *death* was a blessing.

He had been trying for so long to be a ghost, failing miserably and dragging others into danger. Now, he *actually* was a ghost.

There was no better time to go home.

✳ ✳ ✳

Jake waited until he could walk ten yards unaided before booking a flight to Heathrow. His host, Scott, continued to be supportive. He recovered his money and passport from behind the sofa in the office of Hardy's Conveniences.

The passport was a risk. Who knew how far Article SE's influential tentacles wound around England's bureaucracy? It was feasible that they could get an alert to his arrival. But, as was becoming more and more apparent, anything was possible in this world, and sometimes he just had to take a measured risk, so Jake determined to fly home on this passport and place his faith in the sanctity of the Home Office.

Just like he'd done with Logan's parents, he presented

Scott with some money for his troubles and made two more requests. His first request was over the location of somebody who could help him when he returned to England. Jake knew this person would be hard, if not impossible, to locate. Add to that, they were incredibly dangerous; however, this was kind of the point.

Jake was astounded when Scott did his research and handed him his personal cellphone with a number already typed in. "Pulled in a few favors. That number should get you what you want."

Jake made the call, and the voice from his past speared his heart like a cold dagger. But they arranged to meet at Heathrow airport.

The second favor was far simpler. He just needed a ride to the airport, lying low in the back seat so no one saw him.

As they reached the outskirts of Brady Crossing, Jake chanced a look through the window at the mountains towering over this chaotic slice of the world. Swathes of green and brown fields colored the sides, broken occasionally by low clouds rolling across like ghosts.

He saw the beginnings of a familiar dirt track that led off the road.

Smiling, he thought of Celestia's black T-shirt emblazoned with, *Today is a lovely day for you to fuck off.* Jake smiled. *You always did know how to get my attention.* "Stop here."

"Sorry, what?" Scott said.

"Stop. Here."

Scott pulled over. "Why?"

"I like the view." Jake opened the car door.

"I thought you were trying to be discreet!"

"I am. There's no one here. I'll be back in fifteen."

"You're insane."

"Probably," Jake said, stepping from the car. "Actually, *definitely*! However, I never got the chance to say goodbye to someone."

As he headed down the dirt track, he sighed as he recalled Celestia walking backward in front of him, waving him on. "I hope you're not leading me to my death," he said out loud, exactly as he'd done that very day.

Funny you should say that, Frank. He remembered her stopping and pointing to her right. *A lot of people died there —or, at least, as a result of being there.*

At the end of the dirt track, Jake marveled again at the entrance tunneled into the rocks. He was glad to see the iron door closing off the tunnel, and he recalled now Celestia hopping down the steel track that led to it. He also recalled his thoughts that day, which were just as pertinent now. *If you went into that mine now, you may very well end up staying there for good.*

He looked high and watched the sun come in strong over the mountains. The view was stunning and provided a fitting backdrop for him to what he came to do. "Goodbye, Celestia." He smiled. "And no, there is not time to rank Martin Scorsese films."

He was turning to leave when he noticed movement ahead at the mine entrance. He squinted and, shielding his eyes from the sun, surveyed the iron door and the track leading from it.

Nothing. A trick of the light, perhaps?

He waited. *There it was again!* Some movement behind the overturned mining cart.

Never one to shy away from questions that needed answering, Jake approached and started on the metal track leading from the entrance. He kept his hand to his forehead to repel the glare. "Hello?"

He paused to listen.

This time, he heard the movement.

He increased his speed.

A small figure rose from behind the cart.

"Hey!" Jake shouted, holding a hand in the air.

The diminutive figure paused for a moment, probably captivated by the sight of a large man careering toward him, before turning and darting toward the iron door several yards behind him.

"*Wait!*" Jake's recovering gut burned as his heartrate increased. "I don't mean you any harm."

The figure, whom Jake assumed to be a child the closer he got, headed straight to the iron door. Why? It made no sense. They'd be blocked off?

As he drew closer, he saw the door was very crooked and leaned inward. It had clearly come away from its top hinges, creating a yawning gap. Jake's breathing became labored. *Fuck ... how unfit am I?*

A familiar boy turned to look at him with wide eyes. He was emaciated, pale, and sweat and grease glued his lank black hair to his head.

Jake paused at the minecart both stunned and out of breath. "Marston?"

Marston turned, put one foot on the bottom hinges that were still intact, and squeezed through the yawning gap.

"No ..." Jake called out, fighting his breathlessness, to break into another run. "Not in there. It's dangerous."

Jake knew his warning was useless. The ease by which Marston had entered showed he'd been in there before. His ghostlike appearance would also suggest he may have spent a period of time staying there.

Clutching his unhappy stomach wound, Jake reached the door. He sucked in a couple of necessary breaths and peeked through the gap. The leaning door permitted little sunlight into the dark hollows of the mine.

Marston stood a short distance back at the end of a shaft of light.

"Marston." Jake's voice echoed around the mine. "I'm here to help you."

Marston didn't respond. He just stared vacantly in his direction.

Jake recalled Celestia's stomach wound and Logan in a cage. The boy must only have been fourteen, but he remained a dangerous proposition.

But he was *still* just a boy.

"I have no weapons," Jake said. "I *promise* you ... I *guarantee* you'll be safe. Those who hurt your people are in custody."

Marston shook his head.

"It's over. You must trust me. Let me help you. You deserve to live."

"I don't," Marston said.

It was the first time he'd spoken, and it seemed to break his icy, steadfast veneer. His face crumpled, he tilted his head back, and Jake expected him to wail. He didn't. In the end, he lowered his face, and Jake could see his eyes swimming with tears. "My mother?" Marston asked

The boy was desperate. Lying seemed Jake's best option. "Worried about you ... desperate to see you."

Marston started to back away, shaking his head.

"Marston, *wait*!"

The boy disappeared into the darkness.

Shit!

Jake put his foot on the bottom hinges of the iron door in the same way Marston had done. However, their difference in body masses was ridiculous, and there was no way

Jake was squeezing through that yawning gap. Jake leaned forward on the iron door. It creaked and moved. The hinge under his foot buckled as the weighted door pulled at it. The gap widened, slowly at first, then it suddenly sped up. When the door was clearly on the verge of breaking loose, he gritted his teeth. The iron door came down with a thud, and he closed his eyes over the pain that soared through his damaged stomach.

He looked up from where he lay. He couldn't see much, but he could hear Marston's footfalls echoing in the distance. Jake rose to his feet and ran down the metal track that had once carried the cart. The sunlight coming through the open doorway illuminated the passage for a short while, but eventually, Jake broke off right into the darkness.

This was suicide.

"Marston?" he shouted, his voice echoing. He paused to listen for a reply. All he heard was the patter of the fleeing boy's feet.

Ignoring the fatigue, Jake continued his chase, desperately trying to keep to the center of the metal track to not trip over a rail. He also kept his feet high to minimize any risk of low-lying debris.

It soon became too dark to see.

He paused and knelt, shaking his head. What could he do? *Think ... think ...*

The footfalls stopped.

"*Marston?*" he shouted, rising to his feet. He waited for his echo to die.

Nothing.

"*Marston?*" he tried again.

Again, he listened—

"*Help! Help!*" echoed through the tunnel. It had been close though, Jake was certain.

"I'm coming!" With his heart thrashing in his chest, his lungs burning, and his recent scars threatening to burst and bring him to his knees, Jake gave it everything he had.

"Help me!"

The cries became louder and louder, until Jake was almost certain they were coming from beside him rather than in front of him. He turned full circle, but it was far too gloomy, and he could barely decipher the black hollows. *"Marston!* Where are you?"

"Here! I've slipped!"

Jake listened; it sounded like it was coming from his left, below him. He turned and faced that direction. "Marston?"

"I'm falling down a hole!"

He could just about see the blurred line of the track in the gloom. He thought he detected movement there, but with so little visibility, it could easily be his eyes playing tricks on him.

"Help, please! Help! I can't hold on!"

Jake knelt and reached for the track, aiming for that movement in the murk. He wasn't surprised to touch the cold metal of the track and nothing else—

"Please ... I don't know how deep it is! I don't want to be lost down here!"

Jake moved his fingers across the track and felt the warm knuckles of a hand. He reached down and clutched one wrist. Then he located the other hand so he could grab the second wrist.

Then he yanked Marston back up.

* * *

Doubting very much that this had been the only ditch running alongside the track in this decrepit old mine, Jake

211

insisted Marston held his hand as they navigated to the entrance. There had been no need to insist.

Marston clutched his hand for all it was worth and wept throughout the entire cautious exit.

To hear a child in so much pain broke Jake. How many children, every day, were born into worlds as tragic as Marston's? How many children, every *single* day, were forced to endure the kinds of suffering this boy had?

Too *fucking* many.

By the end of the journey, he had to choke back his own tears.

They stepped over the iron door, and the sunlight stung Jake's tearful eyes. He looked down at Marston, who looked back up at him. Apart from some reddening around his eyes from the tears, his face remained pale. Jake tried to release Marston's hand, but the boy responded by gripping harder.

"When did you last eat?" Jake asked, regarding the child's gaunt face.

"I'm sorry about ... Celestia." He blinked rapidly and looked away.

"She's alive. And if she knew you were here in this old mine, you can be sure she'd want to make sure you were okay."

Marston looked back up. His eyes widened. Was a smile threatening to break out on his face? Jake wasn't sure, but he took the hint as a positive sign that maybe Marston could find peace one day.

As they traversed the dirt track, still hand in hand, Jake said, "I lied to you before. About Corrie. Your mother."

"I know she's dead," Marston said, staring straight ahead.

"Yes. How did you know?"

"If she was alive, you wouldn't be."

Jake nodded. Fair point. "I can understand why you'd be upset that it didn't work out that way."

"Not upset. It had to end."

Jake nodded. *Yes, yes it did.* Maybe not in the way it had done, but at least the Nucleus, with its history of blood and tragedy, was no more.

"I thought I wanted to die," Marston said. "I thought I wanted everyone to die. I poisoned my sister, my mother ... I wanted to free them. It was only when I was hanging there that I realized there is no freedom ... only darkness. I'm scared of that darkness." He wept.

"You need to rest; you need to eat. There are people who can help you." Jake led him off the dirt track and toward Scott's car on the road.

Scott exited the car and approached them with his hands in the air. "What the hell?"

Jake nodded. "This is Marston. He needs to eat and drink."

Scott scrutinized the crying boy. "Is he from—"

"Yes. He *was.* Now, he's with you."

"I don't understand."

"This is the penance you were talking about before, Scott."

"I don't understand."

"You do. After you drop me at the airport, you'll do right by this boy. You'll feed him, clothe him, and then you'll find him a home so good that all of this will one day dissolve like a bad dream."

Scott opened his mouth to reply.

Jake stared at him until Scott closed his mouth and nodded.

GONE BUT NOT FORGOTTEN

L ogan pressed the button on his fob, and the garage door rolled up. "Ta-da!"

Celestia surveyed the debris strewn around.

"So?" Logan asked.

Celestia raised an eyebrow. "I like the sign." She pointed at the words emblazoned over the garage door: *Yorke and Reed Motorcycle Repair Shop.*

"And?" Logan prompted.

"And I like the roller door?"

"Well, that did cost a pretty penny! But come on ..." Logan edged backward into the shop with his hands out. "Just look at this." He stumbled over a loose exhaust but managed to keep his footing.

She raised her other eyebrow. "It's a mess."

"Yes. Well, it needs work, but"—he reached for a piece of cloth and ripped it off to reveal a motorcycle—"first customer!"

"Did this customer see inside *here*?"

"No. I met him at his home."

"Good job, really."

Logan scanned the mess. "You're probably right."

"Don't worry. I'll help you tidy it."

Logan pointed at her stomach. "You've got stitches."

"I'm fine."

"You're not. And he's put me under oath to take care of you."

Celestia flinched. The mere mention of Jake unsettled her.

"You know he'll kill me if anything ever happened to you!"

"I don't think you have to worry about that. He's—"

"I do worry." He put his hands on her shoulders. "How many times do I have to tell you? Men like Jake don't die. Not that easily, anyway."

"I hope you're right."

"I am. Why else would I have put his name over my door?"

She pulled away, wiped her tears with the back of her hand, and pointed at the debris. "You need a system."

"What system?"

"I'll tell you where it goes, and you put it there."

"Sounds like a plan."

Less than thirty minutes later, Logan was on his ass in the corner of his still untidy workshop, gulping back air. "I'm not fit enough for this shit."

Laughing, Celestia pulled a rumbling cellphone from her pocket and opened the message from an anonymous number: *Top three Scorsese. Raging Bull ... Taxi Driver ... and?*

She looked up at Logan with tears in her eyes. "You were right."

She watched him rise to his feet, eyes widening, then replied to the message. *Goodfellas.*

215

* * *

Mason, the late Peter Sheenan's treasured dog, woke Piper Goodwin by licking her face.

She pushed the terrier away, and sat upright on the sofa, drying her face with her sleeve. "Who needs an alarm clock?"

Mason bounded away and returned moments later with a tennis ball in his mouth.

"I've *just* woken up!"

Mason whimpered. He'd clearly detected the rejection in her tone.

"After breakfast, I promise."

Her cellphone on the bedside table glowed and vibrated. She reached for it, held it in front of her face, and opened the message from an anonymous caller.

I've got to put some things right. After I do, I'll be back. And we'll be together. J xx

After Piper had stopped crying, she took Mason outside to throw the ball for him.

BETTER THE DEVIL

Bleary eyed following a long flight, Jake wheeled his luggage into the Heathrow arrival lounge. The noise of excited friends and relatives greeted him, as well as insistent taxi drivers thrusting name plaques above their heads.

Jake felt someone brush past him, and his heartrate increased. He calmed himself with a deep breath when he realized it was just an enthused middle-aged woman picking up the pace now; she was a hairbreadth from a loved one.

He sighed. Now that he was back in the UK, paranoia would be the par for the course. He'd be continually looking over his shoulder whenever anyone drew close. After all, powerful people wanted him dead. And if he knew anything about powerful people in the UK, it was they always got what they wanted.

I'll be the exemption to that rule, Jake thought, perusing the plaques.

There it was. A name born from the names of two late colleagues. A tribute, if you like.

Mark Brookes.

His gaze followed the long, slender arms, until he settled on a woman wearing a headscarf over long hair and shades, as if she was avoiding the gaze of the paparazzi. Well, she was infamous, alright. And, just like him, she would also be on the hitlist of some rather unsavory characters, as well as the law.

Is this a mistake?

He turned around the barrier and headed toward her.

Probably.

Do I have a choice?

He pulled up alongside her.

Not really.

"Hello, Mark ... Or do you still prefer Jake, or Frank even? You're a person of many identities."

"As are you, Lacey, as are you."

They didn't look at one another and just stared ahead as more passengers swarmed through customs and into the departure lounge.

"With so many people about, I guess we're safe," Lacey said.

"You and I will never be safe."

"No. I don't suppose we will. I, though, wouldn't have it any other way." She turned to look at him, and he caught her smirk from corner of his eye. "How about you? Do you like it this way?"

Swerving the question, Jake said, "Your hair. Yes, I do like it long. It suits you."

She laughed. "I've missed you, lover."

"Being your lover is not one of my identities. Never was. No one can love you, just like you cannot love them. Anyway, sex is not the reason I contacted you."

"A girl can hope."

Jake guffawed. "Do you hope, Lacey? Do you really feel such things?"

"I long for things, Jake. And I longed for this. Our reunion. *Your* honesty. No one else ever seemed to dare."

"I wonder why. How the hell did you get out of that hospital anyway?"

"With difficulty. It wasn't my easiest challenge. I had to *endure* discomfort first. A lot of discomfort. But it was necessary. Without it, I may not have built the strength to leave."

"That hasn't really answered my question."

"A magician never reveals their secrets."

"You're not a magician, Lacey; you're a killer."

"As are you, Jake, as are you."

Jake looked down. "Yes."

"And that's why you contacted me, isn't it?"

Jake nodded. "I think so."

"Because now that you know what you are, everything is so much easier."

"It hasn't been. It hasn't been easy at all."

"Are you sure about that? Nothing's easier than doing what you know. You've been just fine, Jake. And with my help, I'm sure you'll be just fine again."

"She's dead. Sheila's dead. They killed her."

"I know." Lacey shrugged. "But she was a bitch."

"She was the mother of my son!"

"Yes ... but she was still a bitch."

Jake shook his head. "You really have no fucking empathy."

"You should try it. It really does become very easy then."

"I'll keep my empathy, thanks. We've been standing

around here for long enough. We need to get out of sight, and we need to get ready."

"Sounds good. My place or yours?"

"Well, I don't have one, and I'm not heading into a viper's nest, so let's go for a hotel."

"Jake!" Lacey bit her bottom lip. "Are you sure nothing else is on your mind?"

"The only thing on my mind is my son Frank. Can you help me with that, Lacey?"

"Of course. If you answer me one question. And answer it truthfully."

"I'll try."

She faced him, removed her sunglasses, and looked into his eyes. "Why me?"

Jake shrugged. "Better the devil."

* * *

CONTINUE JAKE'S JOURNEY IN THE NEXT DCI MICHAEL YORKE BOOK, BETTER THE DEVIL ...

Scan the QR to READ NOW!

YOUR FREE DCI YORKE QUICK READ

To receive your FREE and EXCLUSIVE DCI Michael Yorke quick read, *__A Lesson in Crime__*, scan the QR code.

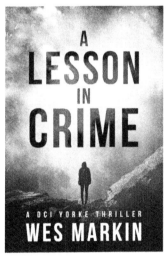

Scan the QR to READ NOW!

Also by Wes Markin
ONE LAST PRAYER

"An explosive and visceral debut with the most terrifying of killers. Wes Markin is a new name to watch out for in crime fiction, and I can't wait to see more of Detective Yorke." – *Bestselling Crime Author Stephen Booth*

The disappearance of a young boy. An investigation paved with depravity and death. Can DCI Michael Yorke survive with his body and soul intact?

With Yorke's small town in the grip of a destructive snowstorm, the relentless detective uncovers a missing boy's connection to a deranged family whose history is steeped in violence. But when all seems lost, Yorke refuses to give in, and journeys deep into the heart of this sinister family for the truth.

And what he discovers there will tear his world apart.

The Rays are here. It's time to start praying.

The shocking and exhilarating new crime thriller will have you turning the pages late into the night.

"A pool of blood, an abduction, swirling blizzards, a haunting mystery, yes, Wes Markin's One Last Prayer for the Rays has all the makings of an absorbing thriller. I recommend that you give it a go." – *Alan Gibbons, Bestselling Author*

One Last Prayer is a shocking and compulsive crime thriller.

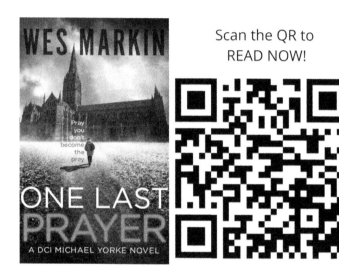

Scan the QR to
READ NOW!

JOIN DCI EMMA GARDNER AS SHE RELOCATES TO KNARESBOROUGH, HARROGATE IN THE NORTH YORKSHIRE MURDERS ...

Still grieving from the tragic death of her colleague, DCI Emma Gardner continues to blame herself and is struggling to focus. So, when she is seconded to the wilds of Yorkshire, Emma hopes she'll be able to get her mind back on the job, doing what she does best - putting killers behind bars.

But when she is immediately thrown into another violent murder, Emma has no time to rest. Desperate to get answers and find the killer, Emma needs all the help she can. But her new partner, DI Paul Riddick, has demons and issues of his own.

And when this new murder reveals links to an old case Riddick was involved with, Emma fears that history might be about to repeat itself...

Don't miss the brand-new gripping crime series by bestselling British crime author Wes Markin!

* * *

What people are saying about Wes Markin...

'Cracking start to an exciting new series. Twist and turns, thrills and kills. I loved it.'

Bestselling author **Ross Greenwood**

'Markin stuns with his latest offering... Mind-bendingly dark and deep, you know it's not for the faint hearted from page one. Intricate plotting, devious twists and excellent characterisation take this tale to a whole new level. Any serious crime fan will love it!'

Bestselling author **Owen Mullen**

Scan the QR to
READ NOW!

The Yorkshire Murders Book 1

THE VIADUCT KILLINGS

WES MARKIN

Acknowledgments

Thanks again to the most supportive group in the world. Without them, little of what you just read would be possible.

My wife, Jo; my children, Hugo and Beatrice; and my entire family. Then, in no particular order: Donna Wilbor, Jenny Cook, Kath Middleton, Karen Ashman, Dee Groocock, Keith Fitzgerald, Claire Cornforth, Carly Markin, Paul Lautman, Holly Sutton, Brian Peone, all of my ARC readers, and those fantastic bloggers who always get behind me – Shell, Susan, Caroline, Jason and Donna. Thank you to Cherie Foxley for the atmospheric cover.

I hope you all join me in Better the Devil when DCI Michael Yorke and Jake Pettman have to reunite with old friends to bring down a powerful and sinister enemy.

Stay in touch

To keep up to date with new publications, tours, and promotions, or if you would like the opportunity to view pre-release novels, please contact me:

Website: www.wesmarkinauthor.com

facebook.com/WesMarkinAuthor

instagram.com/wesmarkinauthor

twitter.com/markinwes

amazon.com/Wes-Markin/e/B07MJP4FXP

Review

If you enjoyed reading **A Rock And Hard Place**, please take a few moments to leave a review on Amazon, Goodreads or BookBub .

Printed in Great Britain
by Amazon